Dear Reader,

If you thought there were no more Oz books after the original fourteen by L. Frank Baum, do we have a marvelous treat in store for you. Ruth Plumly Thompson, named the new Royal Historian of Oz after Baum's death, continued the series for nineteen volumes. And we will be reviving these wonderful books, which have been out of print and unattainable anywhere for almost twenty years.

Readers who are familiar with these books swear that they are just as much fun as the originals. Thompson brought to Oz an extra spice of charming humor and an added richness of imagination. Her whimsical use of language and deftness of characterization make her books a joy to read—for adults and children alike.

If this is your first journey into Oz, let us welcome you to one of the most beloved fantasy worlds ever created. And once you cross the borders, beware—you may never want to leave.

Happy Reading,
Judy-Lynn and Lester del Rey

THE WONDERFUL OZ BOOKS
Now Published by Del Rey Books

By L. Frank Baum

By Ruth Plumly Thompson

*Forthcoming

The Hungry Tiger of OZ

by
Ruth Plumly Thompson

Founded on and continuing the Famous Oz Stories

by
L. Frank Baum

"Royal Historian of Oz"

with illustrations by

John R. Neill

A Del Rey Book
Ballantine Books • New York

List of Chapters

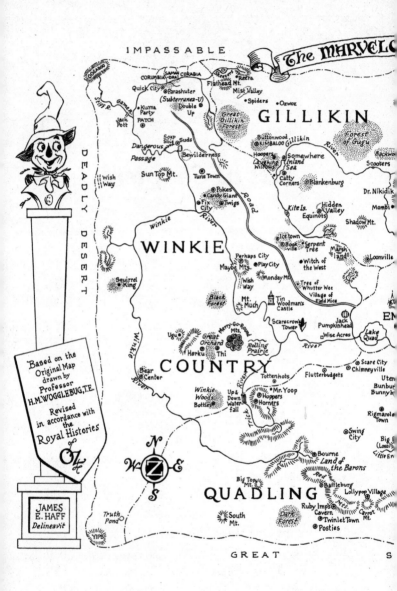

The MARVELO[US]

IMPASSABLE

COGABOO
SAMN CORABIA
CORUMBIA · DRAI
Quick City
Parashuter
(Subterranea-V)
Double Up
Flathead Mt.
Reera
Mist Valley
Spiders
Ozwoz

GILLIKIN

Game
Kuma
Party
Jack Pott
PATCH

Soap Slice
Dangerous Passage
Suds
Bewilderness

Sun Top Mt.
Tune Town

Wish Way

Squirrel King

Bear Center

Ugu
Great Orchard
Herku
Thi

WINKIE

Pokes
Candy Giant
Fix City
Twigs

Perhaps City
Maybe Mts.
Play City
Monday Mt.
Wish Way

Mt. Much

Black Forest

Tin Woodman's Castle

Merry-Go-Round Mts.
Rolling Prairie

COUNTRY

Winkie Wood
Bottles

Up & Down Water fall

Tottenhots
Mr. Yoop
Hoppers
Horners

DEADLY DESERT

Buttonwood
KIMBALOO
Gillikin
Hooper's
Laughing Willows
Catty Corners
Somewhere
Inland Sea
Blankenburg

Forest of Gugu

Backwoo
Scooters

Dr. Nikidik
Mombi

Kite Is.
Equinots
Hidden Valley

Shadow Mt.

Ice town
Boo
ville
Serpent Tree
Marsh lands

Loonville

Witch of the West

Tree of Whutter Wee
Village of Field Mice

Scarecrow's Tower
Jack Pumpkinhead
Wise Acres
Lake Quad

EM

Scare City
Chimneyville
Flutterbudgets

Uten
Bunbur
Bunnyb

Rigmarole Town

Swing City

Big E
(Low)
Little En

Bourne
Land of the Barons

QUADLING

Big Top Mt.

South Mt.

Truth Pond

YIPS

Dark Forest

Red
Baffleburg
Ruby Imps
Cavern
Twinlet Town
Posties

Lollypop Village

Carrot Mt.

GREAT
S

Based on the
Original Map
drawn by
Professor
H.M.WOGGLEBUG,T.E.
Revised
in accordance with
the
Royal Histories
of
OZ

JAMES
E. HAFF
Delineavit

N
W   E
S

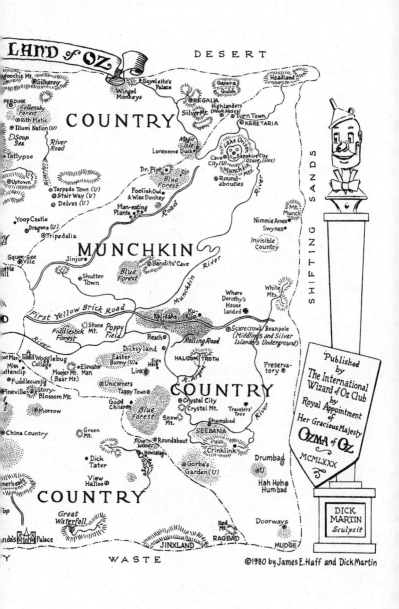

LAND of OZ

DESERT

COUNTRY

Goochie Mt. • Gilkenny
PERDINK
Follensby Forest
Rith Metic
Illumi Nation (U)
Soup Sea
River Road
Tattypoo
Uptown
Torpedo Town (U)
Stair Way (U)
Delves (U)
Yoop Castle
Dragons (U)
Tripedalia
Squee-Gee-Ville
Jinjur

MUNCHKIN

Shutter Town
Blue Forest
Fiddlestick Forest
Stone Mt.
Poppy Field
Wogglebug College
Miss Cuttenclip
Moojer Mt. Man (Bear Mt.)
Elevator Man
Fuddlecumjig
Pineville
Story-Blossom Mt.
Morrow
China Country
merhead
Dick Tater
View Halloo

COUNTRY

Great Waterfall
nda's Palace

WASTE

Gayelette's Palace
Winged Monkeys
Gapers Gulch
Headland
REGALIA
Silver Mt.
Highlanders (Hook Noses)
Turn Town
KERETARIA
Magic Isle
Lonesome Duck
Cave City (U)
Sapphire City (Ozure Isles)
Munchkin Mts.
Dr. Pipt
Ojo
Blue Forest
Round-abouties
Foolish Owl & Wise Donkey
Man-eating Plants
Road
Nimmie Amee Swynes
Invisible Country
Munch
Bandits' Cave
Where Dorothy's House landed
White Mts.
Kalidahs
Ku-Klip
First Yellow Brick Road
Munchkin River
Scarecrow's Beanpole (Middlings and Silver Islanders Underground)
Reach
Rolling Road
Dicksyland
Easter Bunny (U)
Sign Here
HALIDOM
TROTH
Link
Preservatory
Unicorners
Tappy Town
R. Argent
Good Children
COUNTRY
Crystal City
Crystal Mt.
Travelers' Tree
Blue Forest
Snow Mt.
Shamsbad
SEEBANIA
Green Mt.
Pine Woods
Roundabout
Howzatagin
Crinklink
Drumbad
Gorba's Garden (U)
U
Hah Hoh Humbad
Red Mt.
RAGBAD
Doorways
JINXLAND
MUDGE

SHIFTING SANDS

A Map of the Wondrous Lands that lie beyond the Great Desert Barriers of OZ

RIES surrounding OZ

Isle of Dork

Roly-Rogues Is.

The Sea Fairies

NONESTIC

KINGDOM
OF IX

City of Ix

Nole

North Mts.
Roly-Rogues

NOLAND

Aquareine's Palace
(Undersea)

OCEAN

Isle of
Phreex

DESERT

SKAMPAVIA

Valley of
Toy Animals

Valley
of
Pussy-
cats

Valley of
Lost
Things

MERRY
-LAND

Valley
of
Clowns

Palace of
Romance

BLE

COUNTRY

ND OF

OZ

MUNCHKIN

EMERALD
CITY

COUNTRY

COUNTRY

Heelers

Valley
of
Dolls

River

Valley of
Bonbans

Valley of
Babies

Isle
of Mifkets

Pirate Is.

SHIFTING SANDS

LOLAND
ISLAND

Loo Hie

The Enchanted
Forest of Lurla
HEG
AURIEL spot DAWNA
Twi
PLENTA
Isle of Yew

ANDY WASTE

Island of
Civilized Monkeys
ORKLAND

KINGDOM of
SCOWLEYOW

Mt. Mern

Groves
of Trom

Lerd

Caves of the
Daemons

Bumpy
Man

VALLEY
OF MO

(Phunnyland)

Maple Creek

AURISSAU

Fistikins

Jackdaws'
Nest

RIBDIL

Syrup R.

Hartilaf

Based on the
Original Map
drawn by
Professor
H. M. WOGGLEBUG, T.E.

orest
of
rzee

LAUGHING
VALLEY of
HOHAHO

Seventon

Turvyland (V)
Maetta

MACVELT

JUNKUM

BILKON

QUOK

James E. Haff
Del.
Dick Martin
sculp.

MBUMBIA

MULGRAVIA

OCEAN

To Pessim's
Island

King
Anko

©1980 by James E. Haff and Dick Martin

The Hungry Tiger of Oz

CHAPTER 1

The Pasha of Rash

"BURNT AGAIN!" roared the Pasha of Rash, flinging his bowl of pudding across the table. "Vassals! Varlets! Villains! Fetch forth the cook!" At the Pasha's furious words the two Rash Footmen who stood behind his chair, took a running slide down the long dining hall and leaped through the door into the pantry. Several cups crashed against the door as it closed, so it is just as well that they hurried.

As the Pasha reached for a large sauce dish, Ippty, the Chief Scribe of the realm, slipped

1

quietly under the table, where he began jotting down in a little note book each shocking remark about the pudding, making a huge blot whenever a plate broke or a cup splintered to fragments. He had to write pretty fast to keep up with the peppery little Pasha and covered three pages with notes and blots by the time the footmen returned with Hasha, the cook, shivering between them.

"So!" wheezed the ruler of all the Rashes, puffing out his cheeks and glaring at the frightened little man, "Here you are!"

"Am!" choked the poor cook, falling upon his knees. "And may your Excellency live forever!"

"Live forever!" sputtered the Pasha, thumping the table with his fist, "On burnt puddings and raw roasts? It's a wonder I'm alive at all. Do you take me for an ostrich that you serve me lumps of charcoal and call it pudding? Are you a cook or a donkey?"

At this, Ippty lifted a corner of the table cloth and peered out to see what Hasha would say. Then, as the cook made no remark he calmly wrote "donkey," closed the little book and crept cautiously out from his hiding place. There were only three spoons left on the table and he felt pretty sure that these would be flung at Hasha and not at him. He was perfectly right about this and as the last one clattered down upon the head of the luckless cook, Hasha rose, and extending both arms began tremulously:

2

"I did not burn the pudding, Excellency, it was the fire."

"The fire?" raged the Pasha, his eyes fairly popping with indignation. "Do you hear that Ippty, he blames it on the fire. And who tends the fire, pray? Put him out! Fire him! Fizzenpop! Fizzenpop, you old rascal, where are you?"

"The fire shall be put out and the cook shall be fired," muttered Ippty, flipping his book open and scribbling away industriously. This, he could readily do, for the first finger of the Scribe's right hand was a fountain pen, his second finger a long yellow pencil, his third finger an eraser, his little finger a stick of sealing wax and his thumb a fat candle. Ippty's left hand was quite usual, except for the pen knife that served him for a thumb. Blotting the last entry in the book with his cuff, which was

neatly cut from blotting paper, he turned
expectantly toward the door, just as Fizzenpop,
the Grand Vizier, came hurtling through. Being
Grand Vizier of Rash was no easy task and
Fizzenpop had grown thin and bald in the
service of his country.

"What now?" he gasped, pulling on his
slipper and looking anxiously from one to the
other.

"Punish this pudding burner!" commanded
the Pasha angrily. "Put him—"

"In jail!" chuckled Ippty. "In other words
you are to incarcerate the cook." The Chief
Scribe loved long words and knew almost as
many as the crossword puzzle makers.

"But your Highness," objected the Grand
Vizier, pointing his long finger, "the prison is
already overcrowded. Could we not, could we

not cut off his—" Hasha looekd imploringly at Fizzenpop, and the Grand Vizier, clearing his throat, finished hastily, "cut off his allowance instead?"

"No!" thundered Irasha furiously, "I'll be peppered if I will. Prison is the place for him! Out of my sight, scullion!" He waved contemptously at the cook.

"All right," signed Fizzenpop, "I'll put him in the cell with your grand uncle." (The Pasha's grand uncle had been flung into prison for beating the Rash sovereign at chess.) "But remember," warned the Grand Vizier, as Hasha was led disconsolately away by the guards, "remember there is not room for another person. Your Highness will have to find some other way to dispose of prisoners."

"What can I do?" mumbled the Pasha, leaning sulkily on his elbow.

"If you'd take my advice, you'd set them all free," said Fizzenpop calmly. "With half the population in prison, how do you expect to get any work done?"

"Well, why don't they behave themselves then?" demanded the Pasha fretfully. Fizzenpop sighed again, but made no further answer. What use to ask this wicked little ruler why he did not behave himself? Half the arrests in Rash were for no reason at all, and as you are probably puzzling about the location of this singular country, I must tell you that Rash is a small pink Kingdom, in the southwestern country of Ev and directly across the Deadly Desert from the Fairyland of Oz. The Rashes, it is true, are a hasty and hot-tempered race and always breaking out in spots, but they are warm-hearted and generous as well, and with just treatment and proper handling, as loyal subjects as a sovereign could ask for. But Irasha, the present Pasha, was neither just nor wise. He had seized the throne by treachery and was feared and hated by the entire Rash nation, so that one revolution followed another and the realm was in a constant state of uproar. Again and again poor old Fizzenpop would make up his mind to retire, but feeling that he could serve his countrymen better by remaining, had stayed on, enduring the terrible tempers of the Pasha and living for the day when the rightful ruler should be restored to the throne.

"Well, why don't you say something?" growled Irasha, growing irritable at the long silence. "What do other countries do with their prisoners?"

"Why not destroy them?" proposed Ippty cheerfully, before Fizzenpop had a chance to answer. The Chief Scribe was as cruel and merciless as his Master. Irasha had discovered him in a Rash book shop, where he was employed as clerk, and fascinated by his strange hands had raised him to his present important position. "In ancient countries," continued Ippty, sharpening the second finger of his right hand with the thumb of his left, "in ancient

6

countries prisoners were thrown to the wild beasts. Now I call that very neat. No fuss or worry, and practically no expense." Ippty closed his thumb with a pleased smile and looked brightly at the Pasha.

"What!" shrieked Fizzenpop, stamping his foot furiously at the Scribe, "Who ever would think of such a thing?"

"I would," answered the Pasha calmly. "I think it's a very good plan Ippty. But the trouble is," he paused and pushed back his spotted turban, "the trouble is, we have no wild animals. I wish I had a wild animal," sighed Irasha gloomily. With the exception of a few speckled bears, there are no animals of any kind in Rash, and Fizzenpop had just drawn a long breath of relief when Ippty began again.

"But there are plenty of wild animals in Oz, your Highness!" suggested Ippty. "Why not send across the Deadly Desert and get a wild animal from Oz?"

"Why not?" The Pasha straightened up in his chair and looked almost pleasant. "I believe I will," he mused thoughtfully. "An excellent notion, Ippty, for in that case we should not need a prison at all and the expense of feeding the monster would be practically nothing."

"And what's to prevent it from eating us?" demanded Fizzenpop explosively. Up to now he had been able to soften the lot of the Rash prisoners very considerably. He shuddered to think what would happen if Ippty's dreadful

7

plan really were carried out. But Fizzenpop was too wise to openly oppose this rash pair, so he merely shrugged his shoulders. "Well," he sighed folding his arms resignedly, "I hope it works out. I, myself, am too thin to worry, but this beast will probably consider you and Ippty choice morsels!" He rolled his eyes sideways at the fat little Pasha and the still fatter Scribe. "How will a wild animal know the difference between Pashas and prisoners?" he inquired sarcastically. Irasha looked rather uncomfortable.

"We'll have to get a civilized wild animal," he muttered uneasily, "an educated fellow who will eat whom we tell him to and obey the laws of the country."

"And who ever heard of a civilized wild animal?" sniffed the Grand Vizier, with a sour smile.

"I have," declared Ippty, elevating his nose disagreeably. "There are any number of educated wild animals in the Emerald City of Oz. There's the Cowardly Lion, for instance, there's the Comfortable Camel and the Doubtful Dromedary, and there's the Hungry Tiger. How about the Hungry Tiger?" asked Ippty triumphantly.

"Hungry Tiger!" Fizzenpop gave a gasp of dismay, for he had never even heard of such a creature.

"Let's get the Hungry Tiger," yawned the Pasha, who was growing rather sleepy. "He'll

be just the one for us. But are you sure he's tame and harmless, Ippty, and safe to have about?"

"Oh quite!" Ippty assured him quickly. "Why, he wouldn't hurt a baby, his conscience is so tender. That's why he's hungry you know."

"Then what makes you think he will eat the prisoners?" asked the Grand Vizier nervously.

"Well," observed Ippty, scratching his ear with his fountain pen, "when this tiger realizes that it is perfectly legal and lawful to eat prisoners I daresay he will jump at the chance, for in that way he can satisfy his appetite and his conscience at the same time. There are no criminals in the Emerald City, for Ozma, the Queen, is a silly, soft hearted little fairy and never arrests anyone, so the Hungry Tiger will be glad enough to come here and eat our prisoners."

"Ippty is right," puffed the Pasha, rising sitffly from his chair. "Just take a hurry-cane from the stand there, and fetch back this Hungry Tiger, old fellow, and if he won't come fetch him anyway."

"Certainly your Highness," murmured the Scribe, bowing low. "I will start for Oz at once."

"You'll be sorry for this," panted Fizzenpop as the Pasha's pudgy figure disappeared down the pink passageway, and between anger and anxiety the Grand Vizier of Rash began to hop up and down like a jumping-jack.

"What are you dancing," yawned Ippty, "a pepper jig?" And brushing insolently past Fizzenpop, he lifted a hurry-cane from the stand and prepared to depart. First, he lit his right thumb, for it was growing dark; then he tore a page from his note book and wrote, "Carry me to the Emerald City." Unscrewing the top, he thrust this paper carefully down into the head of the cane and screwed the head on again. He had just time to straighten his turban before the hurry-cane, with a whistle and crash, carried him clear out of the castle. Rushing to the window Fizzenpop saw him straddling like some strange bird over Too Much Mountain. The flight of Ippty was not surprising to Fizzenpop for hurry-canes are one of the chief products of Rash and are nearly always used for long journeys. No, it was not Ippty's departure that worried the old statesman. It was the thought of Ippty's return with the Hungry Tiger of Oz. How was he to save his poor prisoners from this dreadful beast?

Pale with anxiety, he rushed into the Rash library and after some searching found what he was looking for—Professor Wogglebug's Encyclopedia of Oz. All his life, Fizzenpop had been so busy straightening out affairs in Rash he had had no time to study adjacent Kingdoms at all and knew little or nothing of the great

fairyland that lay across the desert. Flipping over the pages of the encyclopedia to the T's the Grand Vizier ran his finger down the list till he came to the Hungry Tiger.

"This great and beautiful beast," stated the book shortly, "came to the Emerald City during the first year of Ozma's reign. He has been in all important processions and adventures since then, and is a great favorite with the celebrities of Oz. Because of his sociable nature he prefers life in the capitol to life in the jungle and because of his tender conscience has never been known to devour a live man, fairy, or person."

"Never been known to devour a live person?" shrilled Fizzenpop, dropping the encyclopedia with a bang. "Merciful Mustard! What shall I do now?"

CHAPTER 2
Betsy's Birthday

"WELL!" signed Betsy Bobbin, dropping into one of the royal hammocks and swinging her heels contentedly, "It was the best party I ever had."

"I'm so full of birthday cake, I feel like a sponge," groaned the Cowardly Lion, and sinking down on the grass he began to lick the frosting off his paws.

"No wonder! You had ten pieces," grumbled the Hungry Tiger, settling down sulkily beside him. "Now I call that more than your share, old chap."

"Why shouldn't I have the lion's share,"

13

chuckled the great beast, winking at Betsy. "I notice you ate three roast ducks and all the plum pudding."

"And still I am hungry," complained the tiger, rolling his eyes sadly from side to side. He looked so comical Betsy burst out laughing and the Cowardly Lion fairly roared. Scraps, the Patchwork Girl came running over to see what was the matter. All the celebrities had been invited to Betsy's party and now, in the pleasant dusk, were walking about under the trees in the Palace garden.

Of all gardens in and out of the world, there is none so lovely as Ozma's, and of all fairy cities there is none to compare with the Emerald City of Oz. Its sparkling buildings and shining streets, inlaid with emeralds, its quaint domed cottages and shimmering palace, make it a fitting capitol for this enchanting fairyland. Where but in Oz can animals talk as sensibly as men? Where but in Oz can one live forever, without growing old? Where but in Oz are there Wish Ways and Truth Ponds, Book Mines and Fire Falls and where but in Oz can one find such delightful companions as the Scarecrow and Scraps?

Is it any wonder, then, that Dorothy Gale, who blew to Oz in a cyclone, that Trot and Betsy Bobbin, who arrived in this strange country by way of a shipwreck, have never returned to the real world? Who would? Indeed, these three little mortals live in the Royal Palace itself, with Ozma, the young fairy who rules over the four countries of Oz, and this small sovereign has gathered at her court all the most interesting and unusual people and animals in the realm. And every single one had been invited to Betsy's birthday, so that it took two rooms to hold all the presents, twenty-seven tables to seat the guests and sixty-nine footmen to pass the plates.

"You sit there and tell me you're hungry!" gasped Scraps, snapping her suspender button eyes at the Hungry Tiger. "Why you ate more than anyone. I counted." Scraps, being well stuffed with cotton, never ate at all and had amused herself by keeping strict watch over the others.

"Why Scraps," murmured Ozma reprovingly. She had come up behind the Patchwork Girl and now gently tried to change the subject. No one ever knew what Scraps would say next. Made from a gay patchwork quilt and magically brought to life, this saucy maiden was one of the most surprising people in the castle. But the Hungry Tiger had lived in the Emerald City too long to mind her teasing.

"Of course I'm hungry," he yawned, rolling over on his side. "This party stuff fills me up, but does not satisfy me. What I need is something alive. But don't worry my dear," he added hastily, at Ozma's rather anxious expres-

sion. "I will never devour anyone, for my conscience would not permit it, so I shall be hungry to the end of my days."

"Why don't you have yourself stuffed?" asked the Scarecrow, sitting down in the hammock beside Betsy Bobbin. "Then you would lose this frightful appetite and never be hungry at all. Mighty convenient, being stuffed, old boy. Saves no end of bother and expense." The Scarecrow spoke from experience, for he was himself a stuffed person, having been made by a Munchkin farmer and stuck on a pole to scare away the crows. He had been lifted down and brought to the Emerald City by Dorothy, on her first adventure, and since then has been restuffed and laundered many times. Of all Ozma's advisers, he is the wittiest and most lovable. "Have yourself stuffed," he advised cheerfully, "and use straw like I do."

16

"He stuffs himself from morning till night," snickered Scraps turning a handspring.

> "If he were not so ugly—so yellow and so big
> I'd say he warn't a tiger, but a greedy weedy—"

"Scraps!" Ozma raised her scepter warningly, and the Patchwork Girl dove into a button bush. But almost immediately her mischievous face reappeared.

"Pig!" shouted Scraps defiantly, and looked so funny, peering out of the button bush, that even the Hungry Tiger had to grin.

"I say, though, why *don't* you have yourself stuffed?" asked the little Wizard of Oz, who had just come up. "I've been experimenting with some new wishing powders and might

17

easily wish you out of your jacket and stuff you with sawdust."

"Sawdust!" coughed the Hungry Tiger, sitting up and lashing his tail at the very thought of such a thing, "I should say not. I prefer my own stuffing, thank you."

"So do I," said Betsy, running over to give him a little hug. "You're so soft and comfortable to ride this way."

"But sawdust is very serviceable," urged the Wizard, who was anxious to try his new powders, "and I could stuff you in an hour." The Wizard, by the way, is a mortal like Dorothy and Betsy. Long ago he had been engaged by a circus in Omaha to make balloon flights. But one afternoon, his balloon becoming unmanageable, had flown off—up and away and never stopped till it dropped down in Oz. It was the Wizard who had built the Emerald City and for many years he practiced the trick magic he had learned in the circus. But later, Glinda the good Sorceress of the South, had taught him real magic and he is now one of the most accomplished magicians in all fairy history.

"Better let me stuff you," repeated the Wizard coaxingly.

"No! No! No!" roared the Hungry Tiger, becoming really alarmed at the little man's persistence. "No, I tell you!"

"Well," the Wizard rose regretfully and began to move off, "if you ever change your mind, let me have first chance, will you?"

Betsy's Birthday

"I'm going to change my mind to-morrow."
Sitting down stiffly on a bench opposite the
hammock, Jack Pumpkinhead beamed upon the
company. "It's almost too soft to use," mused
Jack, touching the top of his pumpkin gently,
"so, if you don't mind, I'll not talk any more."

"We don't mind at all," laughed Betsy, while
Dorothy and Trot, who had just joined the
group, exchanged merry winks. Jack was so
amusing that no one could help chuckling when
he was around. He had been made by Ozma,
when she was a little boy, and was almost as
unusual as the Scarecrow. To those not familiar
with Oz history, this may seem a bit strange,
but Ozma once was a little boy, having been
transformed by old Mombi, the witch. And
while she was a little boy she had carved Jack
neatly from wood and set an old pumpkin on
his peg neck for a head. Later he had been
brought to life by mistake and has been living
merrily ever since. Every month or so Jack has
to pick a pumpkin and hollow out a new head
for himself, so that he is constantly changing
his mind, but Ozma has a deep affection for
the queer fellow, and Jack is so odd and jolly
that he is a great favorite in the Emerald City.

"Let's finish off the party with a game of
hide and seek," suggested the Cowardly Lion,
as Jack continued to stare solemnly straight in
front of him. "You're it Betsy!" Giving the little
girl a playful poke, he dashed down an arbored
path, followed helter skelter by all the others.

Even Jack, holding fast to his pumpkin head, ran and hid himself behind a balloon vine. But the Hungry Tiger ran fastest of all, never stopping till he reached the remotest corner of the garden. All this talk of stuffing had made him exceedingly nervous and, with a troubled sigh, he sank down beside a lovely fairy fountain. Here, blinking up at the bright lanterns hung everywhere in honor of Betsy's birthday, he began to think of the good old days when he had roamed the wild jungles of Oz and eaten—well we had best not say what he had eaten!

It was the Cowardly Lion who had coaxed the Hungry Tiger to the capitol. The Cowardly Lion, himself, had come there with Dorothy and the Scarecrow and grown so fond of the place and its people that he had returned to the jungle for his old friend, the Hungry Tiger. And like the Cowardly Lion, the Hungry Tiger had never been able to tear himself away from this dear and delightful city. Indeed life without the love of Dorothy, Betsy and Trot, the trust and affection of little Ozma, and the companionship of all the merry dwellers in the castle, would not be worth a soup bone. So the Hungry Tiger had never gone back, but at times the longing for real tiger food almost overcame him.

"I wonder if stuffing would help," sighed the poor beast, licking his chops hungrily. "I wonder—"

"What?" wheezed an oily voice, almost in

his ear. The Hungry Tiger, supposing himself to be alone, had spoken aloud, and springing up found himself face to face with an ugly, red-faced and exceedingly disagreeable looking stranger. He was dressed in robes of pink, gold embroidered slippers and a simply enormous turban, that wagged from side to side as he talked. An oddly twisted cane swung from his left wrist and as he extended his hand in greeting, the Hungry Tiger jumped back in alarm, for the stranger's thumb was blazing away merrily. It was Ippty, Chief Scribe of Rash, for the hurry-cane had brought him straight to the royal gardens of the Emerald City of Oz.

"Am I addressing the Hungry Tiger of Oz?" inquired Ippty. "And are you still hungry?" he asked eagerly.

"What if I am?" growled the Hungry Tiger, blinking suspiciously at Irasha's singular messenger. "What if I am?"

"Come with me," said Ippty, mysteriously. "Come with me, famous and famished member of the feline family, and you will never know hunger more!"

"Who are you?" rumbled the Hungry Tiger, sitting up and beginning to pant a little from astonishment. "Who are you and what are you doing here?"

"I am Ippty, Chief Scribe of Irasha the Rough, and I am here to offer you an important position at the Court of Rash. Come to Rash,"

begged Ippty, glancing uneasily over his shoulder, for he was not anxious to meet any of the Oz celebrities. "Come, before we are discovered!"

"Rash!" coughed the Hungry Tiger impatiently. "Why should I go to that measly little Kingdom when I am perfectly happy and contented here?"

"Because!" Bending over and splattering the Hungry Tiger with hot candle grease from his thumb, Ippty began whispering earnestly in his ear. At first, the Hungry Tiger's tail lashed and twirled with fury, but as Ippty continued, he grew calmer, and a queer longing crept into his great yellow eyes.

"Stand back fellow," he mumbled crossly, "you will singe off my whiskers, and kindly remove your pencil from my eye."

"But you will come?" Straightening up, Ippty put his bristly hand behind him and regarded the Hungry Tiger expectantly. "Not less than one prisoner a day, sometimes as many as ten," he repeated persuasively.

"Humph!" grunted the tiger, half closing his eyes. Already Ippty's wicked plan was beginning to tempt him. Surely eating criminals would not be wrong, or at least, not so very wrong.

"And these prisoners are dangerous fellows, I suppose?" he asked casually, trying to appear careless and unconcerned about the whole queer business.

"Villains, thieves and robbers, rascally fat rogues who are a menace to the country. By eating them you will be doing Rash a real service," Ippty assured him.

"And where is Rash?" asked the Hungry Tiger, waving his tail inquiringly.

"In the southwestern corner of Ev," answered the Scribe, with a wave that nearly put out his thumb. "And if you are ready, dear beast, we will start at once."

"Ev!" spluttered the tiger, "why that's miles away. I was there long ago, when Ozma, Dorothy and Billina rescued Prince Evardo from the Gnome King. Too far!" yawned the Hungry Tiger, rolling over on the dewy grass. "I'm too tired for such a journey."

"No trip at all!" Ippty touched the hurry cane and in a few words explained its curious mechanism, following it up with such a

23

tempting description of the Rash prisoners that the Hungry Tiger's appetite got the better of his conscience.

"I'll go," he agreed gruffly, "but only for a few days, remember." Ippty said nothing, but smiled wickedly to himself. Then, stuffing the directions for their return into the hurry cane, he sprang upon the Hungry Tiger's back. Next instant, in a flash of fire and smoke, they had disappeared from the garden.

"What was that?" gasped Dorothy, clutching Ozma by the sleeve. Both little girls, crouched behind a button bush, had seen the strange flash.

"Lightning, I guess!" shuddered Ozma. "Let's run back to the castle, Dorothy. A thunder storm's coming!"

CHAPTER 3

The Hungry Tiger in Rash

IT WAS night time when Ippty and the Hungry Tiger arrived at the pink palace. Travelling by hurry cane is a hair-raising experience, let me tell you. Showing the breathless beast to a luxurious apartment, the Chief Scribe hurried off to the Pasha, and until long after midnight the two whispered and conferred together. Of course it was about the Hungry Tiger that they talked.

"A saucy, but serviceable brute," finished

Ippty, blowing out his thumb, "and he will require watching, Your Highness, for would not a tiger fed on criminals grow dangerous?"

"We'll lock him up in the prison court-yard," declared Irashi, rubbing his hands gleefully together, "then there'll be no chance of his running away or chewing off our heads. Good work, old Butter-tub, I'll raise your wages for this." And clapping his Chief Scribe on the back, Irashi tumbled into bed and was soon snoring loudly.

The Hungry Tiger did not find falling asleep so easy. Already he regretted his rash action in coming with Ippty. Padding up and down the big bedroom, he began anxiously to reflect upon the duties of his new office. Was it right or wrong to eat the Rash criminals? What would Ozma think if she knew? The gentle face of the little fairy kept rising reproachfully between him and the thought of the fat and tempting prisoners. "I'll stay just a few days," groaned the poor tiger at last, trying to put Ozma out of his mind, "and only eat the very worst and wickedest ones. I hope they'll not taste too bad," he yawned, sinking down wearily on the soft pink rug, "nor have too many knives and swords in their pockets. Hah, hoh, hum!" With a great yawn, the tired tiger rolled over and fell into a troubled sleep.

A shrill blast of trumpets wakened him next morning and a few moments later Ippty came to conduct him to the Pasha. Irashi had craftily arranged to receive the Hungry Tiger in the prison courtyard, and surrounded by the Rash Guardsmen, with Fizzenpop standing anxiously at his side, he waited for the tiger to appear. The walk from the palace to the prison was not long, but it gave the Hungry Tiger quite a glimpse of the country and the people. The palace and all of the cottages and stores were of pink stone. Pink trees lined the pink marble walks and even the sky had a rosy glow. The Rashers, themselves, hurrying to and fro in their tremendous flapping turbans, oddly quilted robes and soft pink slippers, seemed pleasant enough fellows and again the Hungry Tiger's conscience began to trouble him. But it was too late to turn back now, so he stalked uncomfortably after Ippty. The prison itself looked quite like a wing of the pink palace and unsuspectingly the Hungry Tiger passed through the great golden gates and into a high walled court.

"Ah hah!" exclaimed Irashi, as he advanced majestically to the center of the court-yard. "So here he is at last, the famous and famished tiger of Oz. And in uniform, too. Is it not splendid that the future jailer of Rash should wear stripes," chuckled the Pasha, poking Fizzenpop playfully in the ribs. "Even now our prisoners will go behind the bars—after they are eaten," he whispered hoarsely, fearing Fizzenpop might not get the joke. Ippty burst into a loud roar, but the Grand Vizier, after

27

one look at the huge figure of the tiger, began
to tremble from top to toe. The Hungry Tiger,
himself, was not at all pleased with his
reception.

"Are you laughing at me" he growled, lashing
his tail and showing so many teeth the Rash
Guardsmen took to their pink heels. "Are you
laughing at ME?"

"No! No, certainly not," grunted Irashi,
moving hurriedly toward the gates. "I hope you
will be most comfortable and happy here." At
each word, Irashi took a great leap, followed
closely by Ippty and Fizzenpop. By the time he
finished his sentence and before the Hungry
Tiger realized what was happening, all three
were on the other side of the gates and the
tiger, himself, was locked fast in the courtyard.

"Stay there, you saucy monster," puffed

Irashi, shaking his scepter playfully, and taking Fizzenpop by one arm and Ippty by the other, he waddled off, leaving the Hungry Tiger to reflect upon his folly. First he hurled himself again and again at the golden gates, then he ran round and round the prison yard examining every inch of the high walls. But it was useless. There was not so much as a chink in the marble blocks. Raging with anger at Irashi and disgusted with himself for being so easily caught, he crouched down in a gloomy corner of the yard to think. All choice in the matter of eating the Rash prisoners was now removed, for, as he sadly reflected, there would probably be nothing else to eat. But eating prisoners, when you are free and happy, and eating prisoners because there is nothing else are entirely different matters and already half the pleasure was gone from the experiment. How was he to escape from this miserable little monarch? Would Dorothy and Betsy miss him? Why, oh why, had he not listened to the voice of his conscience or even had himself stuffed, as the Wizard suggested?

Blinking his eyes mournfully, the Hungry Tiger began to feel sorry not only for the Rash prisoners, but dreadfully sorry for himself, for was he not a prisoner, too? He had plenty of time to feel sorry, for not a soul came near him all day—not even a Rash mouse. There was a tub of water in the corner of the yard, but nothing to eat, and as the shadows grew longer and longer the poor tiger grew hungrier and hungrier. Betsy's party seemed years ago and when, toward evening, shrill screams from the wall announced the approach of Irashi and the guards, he looked up almost hopefully to see whether they were bringing a prisoner. They were. Propped up between two guards, and advancing most unwillingly, was a tall turbaned figure.

"Here!" shouted Irashi, leaning far over the wall, "here is your supper. Eat this rogue at once. He has wakened me from my sacred nap with his horrible howling."

"I suppose I'll have to," mumbled the Hungry Tiger uncomfortably to himself, and growling to keep his courage up and his conscience down, he advanced toward the wall just as the guardsmen dropped the luckless Rasher over. He landed lightly on the balls of his feet and after one look at the Hungry Tiger pulled his turban over his eyes and began to screech with terror.

"Eat him up! Shut him up! What's the matter, have you no teeth?" bawled Irashi covering his ears.

"I never dine till ten o'clock," answered the Hungry Tiger stiffly. He was not going to be bullied by the wretched little sovereign of Rash. "And I never eat until I am alone," he growled raising his roar above the wails of the prisoner.

"Suit yourself," grumbled Irashi. But secretly he was disappointed. To watch the Hungry Tiger devour the prisoner would have been a real treat for the wicked little Pasha. Covering both ears to drown the poor fellow's doleful yells, he scrambled down the steps on the other side of the wall. "We'll return later to see if he is eaten," puffed the little Pasha, turning back toward the castle, and the guardsmen, exchanging uneasy glances, clanked after him. As soon as they were alone, the Hungry Tiger approached the prisoner.

"Would you mind stopping that noise?" he begged earnestly. "You're really spoiling my supper."

"Your supper?" gulped the Rasher, trembling violently, "Do you expect me to submit to eating without a sound?"

"Well, I wish that you would," sighed the

31

tiger hopefully. "I never cared for music with my meals. Now don't be frightened, I won't hurt you—much. If you were not so tall, I'd swallow you whole."

"Oh!" groaned the prisoner falling upon his knees, "Have you no heart? No conscience? Are you really cruel enough to devour a poor fellow like me?" At each word, the Hungry Tiger recoiled a bit further.

"But what can I do? I've nothing else to eat and it is the Rash law that you should perish. By the way, what was your crime?" he asked sadly. Now that the time for eating a live man was at hand, he found himself curiously disturbed.

"I'm a singer," began the prisoner, in a choked and frightened voice. "This afternoon, hoping to earn a few Rash pence, I stopped beneath the palace balcony and—" Straightening up and throwing out his chest, the singer burst into tears and song, mingling them so thoroughly the Hungry Tiger was soon crying like a baby himself. Without the tears, the song went something like this:

> "Oh why must lovely roses die?
> Oh why, snif! snif! Oh why, say why?
> Oh why must hay be cut and mown
> In its first hey-day? Groan, snif, groan!
>
> And why must grass be trodden down
> And trees cut up to build a town?

32

The Hungry Tiger in Rash

Should little lambs grow into chops
And hang around in butcher shops?
No! No! I weep, it is too sad.
Snif, snuffle, snif, I feel so sad!"

"So do I!" roared the Hungry Tiger. "Stop! Stop! I am positively ill. What's that?" That was a large bunch of bananas. It came whistling over the wall, followed by three onions, a sausage, a squash pie and a head of cabbage.

"They always throw things when I sing," sobbed the singer, drying his eyes on his pink sleeve.

"Pass me that sausage," gulped the Hungry Tiger in a faint voice.

"Are—aren't you going to eat me?" stuttered the sad singer, offering the sausage fearfully and jumping back as if he expected the tiger to snap off his arm. Between bites, and the sausage took only two, the Hungry Tiger shook his head.

"Not now," he answered wearily. "I might have swallowed *you*, but that song! Never! A man full of music like that would ruin my digestion. How's the pie?"

"Squashed," said the singer, in a depressed whisper. "Try the onions." He held them out hopefully, but the Hungry Tiger only shuddered.

"Eat them yourself," he advised gloomily, "you seem to enjoy crying." Reaching for a banana, the Hungry Tiger ripped off the skin

33

and swallowed it whole. Three more, he treated in the same reckless fashion. Then licking his whiskers, he regarded the sad singer reproachfully. "You may go now," he said gruffly. "Your singing is outrageous, but you are neither wicked enough to satisfy my conscience nor fat enough to satisfy my appetite. Go—go—before—"

"But how can I go," moaned the singer, waving despairingly at the high walls. I do not know whether his tears were from grief, gratitude or onions. (He had eaten all three by this time.)

"Well, you can't stay here," rumbled the tiger anxiously, "for you're supposed to be eaten."

"I'll hide," muttered the prisoner, glaring around wildly. But there was no place in the whole pink yard where he could conceal himself. Round and round tore the worried Rasher and round and round after him nosed the Hungry Tiger and, just as the moon rose up over the pink turrets of the palace, they discovered a loose block in the stone pavings. Scratching frantically with his powerful claws the Hungry Tiger managed to dig up the whole block and dragging it aside found a small damp underground chamber.

The sad singer was overjoyed, when he peeped into the dark hole, for he had become very nervous, in his fear that the tiger would soon decide to eat him. To tell the truth, the Hungry Tiger was glad himself. The sad singer did not look very good to eat.

"There!" grunted the Hungry Tiger, thrusting the singer in and throwing some bananas and a head of cabbage after him. "Be quiet and whatever you do, *don't sing!*" He had just pushed the block back, leaving a small crevice to give the prisoner air, when Irashi and Ippty appeared upon the wall.

"Ah! He has eaten him!" cried Irashi rapturously, and clapping his hands like a child, be began to address the Hungry Tiger in most affectionate terms, promising him a dozen prisoners upon the morrow. But the Hungry Tiger merely turned his back and gazed solemnly up at the moon, and seeing nothing was to be

got out of him, Irashi and his wicked scribe tiptoed off to bed, well pleased with the new jailer of Rash. The Hungry Tiger himself, in spite of a horribly hollow feeling (what is a sausage and four bananas to a tiger?) soon fell asleep. And perhaps because he had done nothing to trouble his kind old conscience, he dreamed that he was safely back in the Emerald City with dear little Ozma of Oz.

CHAPTER 4

The Vegetable Man
of Ox

WE shall have to leave the poor Hungry
Tiger in the jail yard of Rash and take
a peep at what is going on in the Emerald City
of Oz. It will be something exciting, I am sure.
One never can guess what will happen next in
the Fairyland of Oz.

"Red ripe tomatoes! Red ripe tomatoes!
  Fresh straw-burees! Fresh straw-burees!
Ripe red tomatoes, fine new potatoes
  Salad! Cress and peas! Fresh straw-burees!"

"Strawberries!" exclaimed Betsy Bobbin in delight, and running to the palace window, looked up and down the garden to see where the voice was coming from. It was so like old times in the States it made Betsy homesick. "Why, I never heard a huckster calling around here before," thought Betsy. "I believe I'll buy some for breakfast and surprise Ozma." Fastening the last button on her blue frock, she skipped out of the room, down the stairs and into the garden, following the sound of the husky voice. Sometimes it seemed to be quite near, at other times to come drifting back to her from a great distance and before long Betsy was perfectly breathless from darting to and fro. But at last a sharp turn in the path brought her right upon the owner of the voice. It was a Vegetable Man, sure enough, his small hand cart piled high with fresh greens and rosy strawberries.

"I'll take a box of berries, please," panted Betsy, and standing on her tiptoes, she pointed to a very large and tempting one.

"Certainly Miss," said the Vegetable Man, and handing her the box stood smiling and bowing in the roadway. But instead of taking it Betsy gasped and put both hands behind her.

"Now don't be skeered," said the Vegetable Man softly. "I know I'm an odd one, but you'll get used to me. Try to get used to me," he begged coaxingly. Betsy thought it would take a long time, but he seemed so earnest that she took a long breath and looked at him again. His face was red and smooth as a beet. Queer, rootlike whiskers sprouted raggedly from the bottom, curious celery leaf hair waved excitedly from the top, while a turnip nose and two tall corn ears gave him a most roguish and inquisitive expression. His body was more like an enormous potato than anything else and his arms and legs were long, wiry roots of some coarse vegetable fibre.

"Well?" asked the Vegetable Man anxiously, as Betsy finished her inspection. "Can you stand me at all?"

"I—I think you're pretty interesting," confessed Betsy, who was an exceedingly polite and kind hearted little girl.

"Am I?" beamed the stranger, rubbing his twig like hands together, "Well! Well! I'm glad to hear you say that, for it's just what I've been thinking myself. But I was not always like this, my dear." The Vegetable Man's blue eyes were the only natural feature about him and they twinkled so merrily above his turnip nose that Betsy began to feel quite drawn to him. "I was a Winkie," he confided mysteriously, "and sold fresh vegetables to all the royal families in Oz. But each night when I returned to my farm, there were vegetables left in my cart, so young, so fresh, so fair, I could not let them die, so I ate them," he continued dreamily. "And bit by bit I turned to the figure you see before you. But I'm quite used to myself now and can still carry on my business. In fact—Oh, spinach!" The Vegetable Man interrupted himself crossly. "Spinach and rhubarb!"

"Why what's the matter?" asked Betsy in surprise, for he had put down the strawberries and was tugging with all his might at his left foot, which presently came up so violently, he sat down hard in the road.

"Would you mind walking on as we converse?" puffed the Vegetable Man, picking up the box of berries and springing nimbly to his feet. "I take root if I stand still," he said apologetically. "It would be awfully inconvenient to become rooted to this spot, and there's no telling what I'd grow into."

"Why don't you wear shoes?" asked Betsy, trotting along beside the cart and almost forgetting about the strawberries in her extreme interest.

"I never thought of that," mused the Vegetable Man, looking down ruefully at his huge twisted feet. "Do you s'pose I could ever find any shoes to fit, Miss—Miss? What is your name, now? Mine's Green, Carter Green, but most folks call me Carter."

"Mine's Betsy Bobbin, but I think I'd better go back now or I'll be late for breakfast." Stopping reluctantly, Betsy reached for her box of berries, and as she had brought no money she slipped a small emerald ring into the Vegetable Man's hand. At first he refused to take it, but as the little girl insisted and assured him she had dozens more like it, Carter slipped the ring into the leather pouch he wore round his neck.

"I've a stone something like this," he told her and, hopping up and down to keep from taking root, he fumbled in the pouch till he brought out a large square ruby. "Found it in a potato," continued Carter, as Betsy turned it over and over in her hand. "Not in any I raised myself, but in one of a lot I bought from a gypsy. Like it?" Betsy nodded emphatically, for not even in Ozma's crown itself had she seen a more dazzling jewel. There was a small R cut in one of the flat sides of the gem and the ruby itself blazed and sparkled in the sunshine and fairly made Betsy blink.

"But I wonder what the R stands for?" she murmured softly.

"Raspberries, I guess," chuckled the Vege-

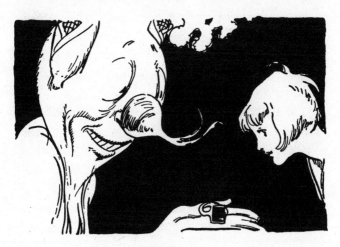

41

table Man, putting the ruby back into his pouch. "Raspberries, rhubarb or radishes. Have a radish, my dear Miss Betsy?"

"Oh, no thank you, and I really must go now." Holding the strawberries carefully, Betsy smiled up into the pleasant face of Mr. Carter Green. He was so curious and exciting she hated to leave him, but Dorothy and Ozma would surely think her lost, so with a little skip she turned about. "Don't forget the shoes," she reminded him gaily. "Goodbye! Good—gracious!"

"Hold tight, Betsy! Hold tight! Celery and cinnamon! What's the matter here?" Seizing his cart with one hand and the little girl with the other, the Vegetable Man teetered backward and forward in the road. And no wonder! It had suddenly ripped itself loose and was rushing along at such a rate that trees and fences simply whizzed past. Betsy's hat blew off at the first curve and strawberries, beets and bananas flew out in every direction.

"I—was—afraid—of—this!" panted the Vegetable Man. "I—should—have—taken—the —regular—road!"

"Isn't this a reg-u-lar—road!" called Betsy, hanging on to Carter with both hands. "What's—it—doing?"

"Winding!" shrieked the Vegetable Man, trying to keep the rest of his vegetables from bouncing out of the cart. "It's—a—winding— road—Betsy! Shut—your eyes, quick!"

Betsy was glad enough to obey, for the road was going round like a top, round and round like a merry-go-round, in and out of trees, past lakes and forests, till the whole world tilted topsy-turvey. Then as suddenly as it had started to wind, it stopped, and when Betsy opened her eyes she was sitting on a small sand dune entirely surrounded by cabbages. A short distance away lay the Vegetable Man, still clutching his cart. While Betsy was still trying to catch her breath, Carter jumped up and shading his eyes looked in all directions.

"Well, it's gone," he exclaimed ruefully and he was perfectly right. There was no sign of a road anywhere. It had cruelly gone off and left them in a wilderness of sand and scorched desert grass.

"Why, I never knew there was a winding road near the Emerald City?" Betsy jumped up indignantly. "Where did it come from?"

"Never can tell," sighed the Vegetable Man, beginning to collect his cabbages. "They just come and go, these winding roads of Oz; pass themselves off as regular roads till they catch a few travellers and you never can tell where they will take you."

"Well, I don't think much of this place," groaned Betsy, rubbing her elbow, which had been severely skinned during the journey over the winding road.

"Then let's go some other place," proposed the Vegetable Man cheerfully. All the strawberries and bananas had spilled out of the cart, but there were plenty of cabbages and apples left and he was busily rearranging these all the time he was talking to Betsy. "Have a cabbage?" he invited pleasantly. "Nothing like cabbages for a ship-wreck."

"It was something like a ship-wreck," mused Betsy thoughtfully. "But I'd rather have an apple, if you don't mind. Do you think we'll ever find the way back to the Emerald City, Mr. Green?"

Carter nodded so vigorously his celery tops waved for moments afterward and, handing Betsy an apple, he pointed off toward the south.

"It's somewhere in that direction, and if you are ready we'd better start." Carter looked a little anxiously at his feet to see if he was taking root, but the ground was too dry and sandy. "I don't believe even I would grow in this kind of soil," he muttered uneasily. "It's hot enough to scorch a fellow. Wish I had a pair of shoes right now. Come, let's move on!"

Lifting Betsy on top of the cabbages, the Vegetable Man grasped the handles of his cart and started on a run across the sandy wasteland. It was not unpleasant, rattling along in the queer little cart and the morning was so brisk and fine Betsy soon began to enjoy herself. "Won't Dorothy and Ozma be surprised when I come rolling up to the castle in this," she chuckled merrily to herself, "and won't they stare when I introduce the Vegetable Man!

Why, he's almost as int'resting as Tik Tok and more fun. I wonder if everybody who eats too many vegetables grows celery tops and corn ears? Oh Mr. Green! Mr. Gr—een!" But the cart wheels were going round with such a squeak, grind and rattle that he did not hear her and Betsy sensibly decided to save this important question for another time.

She had just finished her second apple when the Vegetable Man stopped with a jerk. A rude sign stuck up in the limb of a crooked tree had caught his attention. "Quick Sand," said the sign, "Go Slow!"

"Oh spinach!" exclaimed the Vegetable Man, wiping his face on a stray salad leaf. "Oh spinach!"

"Do you 'spose it's very quick sand?" asked Betsy, leaning far over the side of the cart.

"We'll soon find that out." Taking an apple, Carter flung it as far as he could. But horrors! No sooner had it touched the sand than it disappeared as suddenly as one drop of dew on a frying pan.

"It's a good thing you stopped," shuddered Betsy, "or we'd have been swallowed up."

"Down," corrected Carter gloomily. "Looks like pretty quick sand to me, Betsy. Guess we'll have to turn back." Mournfully, Carter began bringing the cart about. The way they had come was so rough and uneven that he hated the thought of travelling over it again.

"But that won't take us to the Emerald City,"

objected Betsy, beginning to grow a little anxious. "Maybe we could find a path if we looked carefully enough."

Jumping out of the cart, Betsy climbed a small dune. But as far as the eye could reach there was nothing but sand. Sand, sand, sand, shimmering dizzily in the sunlight, with not a tree, path or even a blade of grass to break the monotony. With a sigh, Betsy started down the dune. She had gone about half-way, when a big, newspaper-wrapped package made her pause. It was covered with a queer writing that she could not understand, but looked so interesting she hastily shook it open. Imagine her astonishment when a huge pair of sandals tumbled out. They were cut from white leather, had silver buckles and were almost large enough for a giant.

"Why, I believe they'd fit Carter," murmured

Betsy in pleased surprise. "How lucky I found them." Gathering the sandals up in her arms, she ran down to the Vegetable Man. He was almost as pleased as she was, for the trip across the dry desert had already begun to curl up his toes and, while she climbed back into the cart, he sat down to try them on. They were a bit long, but just the right width and as he fastened the first one he noticed two words cut into the buckle.

"Quick Sandals," murmured Carter under his breath. "Now what may that mean?" But he was in such a hurry to be off, he did not stop to puzzle it out and drawing on the other sandal, jumped excitedly to his feet. "Now I won't be taking root!" he cried joyfully. "Now—" A strange look came into his mild blue eyes, and next instant he had sprung into the air like a jack rabbit. "Help!" screamed the Vegetable Man. "Spinach! Tomatoes! Turnips and Cress!" And while Betsy stared at him in dismay and growing alarm, he sprang twice as high as he had in the first place, seized the handles of the cart and started on a gallop for the quick sand.

"Oh stop! Oh stop!" wailed the little girl frantically. "Stop, Carter, stop!" But he paid not the smallest attention to her. Now they were on the quick sand itself and Betsy, with a scream, buried her face in the cabbages. But the rattle and bump of the cart continued and, concluding that she could not be swallowed up yet, she ventured to raise her head. What she saw this time was so much worse that she had not even courage to cry "Stop!" They had crossed the quick sand and were right on the edge of the Deadly Desert. Betsy well knew the look of this dread wilderness that surrounds the Fairyland of Oz and she knew also that contact with its burning sands meant instant destruction. She tried to signal to the Vegetable Man, but the cart was bumping and bouncing so terribly, it was all she could do to keep from falling out. Carter himself was running as if his life depended upon it, his celery tops waving wildly and his corn ears rustling in the wind. With a choked sob, poor little Betsy shut her eyes and dropped face down among the vegetables.

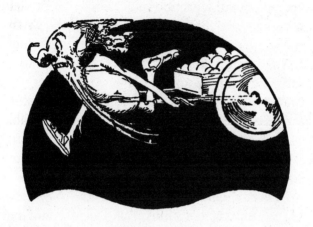

CHAPTER 5
Prisoners in Rash

BETSY never had been destroyed in her life, so she was not at all sure how it would feel. A hot dry wind whistled through her hair, and above the rumble of the wheels she could hear the sharp gasps of Carter Green. Then everything stopped at once, the cart, the burning wind and the hoarse breathing of the Vegetable Man.

"He's destroyed," cried Betsy despairingly, "and now it's my turn." Closing her eyes and trying hard to be brave, Betsy waited for destruction. But nothing at all happened, and

49

after a few terrible moments, she sat up and peered timidly around her. On a pink mile stone, beside the cart, sat the Vegetable Man, staring across the Deadly Desert. Following his startled gaze, Betsy saw two white objects, skipping merrily toward the sky line. It was the sandals. Just as she had made sure of it, they disappeared in a final spurt of speed and sand.

"Why, how did they get off?" stammered Betsy, blinking with astonishment.

"Took themselves," groaned the Vegetable Man, rubbing his shins, "and glad I am that they did. But they've brought us safely across the quick sand and Deadly Desert and here we are!"

"Yes," agreed Betsy resignedly, "here we are, but where are we? *I* didn't know they were quick sandals. Did they really run away with you?" Carter nodded and rose stiffly to his feet.

"I must say Betsy," grunted the Vegetable Man, "I prefer to run myself and not be carried off by a frisky pair of shoes. After this I'll do my own kicking, my own stopping and my own starting, thank you! And we'd better start right away or everything will be spoiled." He looked anxiously into the cart and, jumping out, Betsy began to help him dust and rearrange the vegetables. They had been sadly jolted about by the trip.

As it was impossible to go back across the desert without the quick sandals, they sensibly decided to go forward. There were two roads, stretching invitingly ahead and after a short debate they took the left one.

"This reminds me a little of the Rose Kingdom," mused Betsy, as they walked along under the flowering trees. "Everything is pink, Carter, have you noticed, even the clouds."

"Why there's a pink castle!" cried Carter, with an excited wave. "Maybe we can sell the King of this country some cabbages and maybe he can tell us the way back to the Emerald City."

"Perhaps we'd better try some of the cottages first," suggested Betsy uneasily. In her many adventures she had discovered that kings were not always safe nor agreeable persons to deal with.

"No! No!" insisted Carter, "Kings make the best customers, Betsy. Compliment and flatter 'em and sell 'em the whole cart load, that's my way. Jump in and I'll run you right up to the castle."

Lifting her gaily into the cart, he started briskly down the pink lane calling, "Cabbages! fresh cabbages!" at the top of his vegetable voice. The lane led straight into a bright pink city and Betsy soon grew so interested in its tall turbaned citizens and queer cottages and shops that she forgot to worry about the King. She remembered afterward the scared glances of some of the townsmen, as they went rattling by, but at the time neither she nor Carter noticed anything amiss and the Vegetable Man never stopped till he reached the pink palace itself. As Carter paused under a balcony and began lustily calling his wares, a window just below was flung up violently and a turbaned head wagged warningly over the sill.

"Go away! Go away!" quavered an old man, in a frightened voice. "The Pasha is in a terrible temper. Go away! Go away, rash mortals, I beg of you!"

But the Vegetable Man only laughed. "Wait till he's seen my cabbages," called Carter, holding one up proudly. "Wait—" And they did not have long to wait, let me tell you, for at that precise moment the Pasha of Rash rushed out upon the balcony—the Pasha, himself, and Ippty, Chief Scribe of the Realm, for Betsy and the Vegetable Man had, as you have probably guessed already, run straight into that peppery country.

"Good morning!" cried Carter, pleasantly, in no wise alarmed by the fearful frown of the Rash Ruler. "Permit me to observe that your Highness is beautiful as a banana and fragrant as an onion. And I am here to serve you. Let me serve your Majesty with a fresh young cauliflower, a bunch of beets or this handsome cabbage!" Carter held up the cabbage coaxingly.

"A cabbage! A cabbage!" choked Irashi, turning perfectly pink with passion. "How dare you offer me a cabbage?" So angry that further speech was impossible, he turned furiously to

Ippty, waving his arms and sputtering like a motor cycle.

"Begone, pernicious peddlers," ordered the Chief Scribe, pointing his fountain pen finger sternly at the two travellers. "Begone at once from Rash."

Three drops of ink fell upon Betsy's upturned nose and, thoroughly alarmed, the little girl sprang out of the cart and tried to pull Carter away.

"Hurry up! Hurry up!" she begged breathlessly, "Let's run." But already the Vegetable Man had tarried too long and was firmly rooted to the spot. And while he tugged wildly at one foot and then the other and Betsy jumped up and down with fright and impatience, Ippty leaned over the balcony. A closer inspection of the Vegetable Man proved so astonishing to the Chief Scribe that he nearly fell over the railing.

"He has corn ears!" yelled Ippty shrilly, "and a turnip nose. Look! Look at the monstrous creature!" Thus urged, Irashi, himself, peered over the railing. Perceiving in a moment what had happened to Carter, he began to stamp and shriek with anger.

"How dare you plant your feet in my best flower beds," howled Irashi. "Call out the Guards! Throw them to the tiger. Salt! Vinegar! Mustard! Pepper!" At each shriek a Rash Guardsman dashed out of the palace, and before Carter could jerk himself loose he and Betsy were overpowered.

"He can't help taking root," protested Betsy indignantly. "He's a Vegetable Man."

"Aha! Now we are getting to the root of the matter," snickered Ippty harshly. "And what right has a Vegetable Man in Rash, young lady?"

"Root him up! Throw him to the tiger. Vegetable Man! Vegetable Man, indeed!" roared Irashi, stamping one foot and then the other.

"Tiger!" groaned Carter. "How perfectly carnivorous. Of course," he added turning quickly to Betsy. "It wouldn't hurt me, for I have no feelings, but it will ruin my business. Spare me!" he cried, waving his arms imploringly up at the balcony. "And if you cannot spare me, spare my potatoes, my cabbages and fresh young beets. And spare this lovely little lady from Oz!"

"We'll spare you, all right," wheezed Irashi grimly.

"He'd make excellent soup, your Highness!" suggested Ippty, glancing down sideways at the Vegetable Man, but Irashi shook his head.

"No! No! The tiger shall have him," declared Irashi stubbornly. "It'll be a nice change for him Ippty, a little green with his dinner." Irashi was so pleased with his joke that he winked down at Betsy. But the little girl stamped her foot angrily.

"You'd better let us go, or Ozma of Oz will capture your whole kingdom. We're important people back in Oz!" shouted Betsy defiantly.

"Perhaps the girl is right," ventured Fizzen-pop, who had stolen anxiously out upon the balcony. "What harm have they done? Let them go, I beg!"

"No!" With a determined wag of his turban, Irashi signaled to the Guard and flounced back into the palace.

"Don't cry, Betsy," begged the Vegetable Man. The Guards had at last jerked him loose and were marching the two across the gardens. "This tiger will probably eat me first and I'm so tough he'll choke to death and you can run away."

"Well, I wish I had never found those quick sandals," wailed the little girl. "It was the quick sandals that brought us here, Carter, and I don't believe Ozma knows about this dreadful country at all. Couldn't you please let us go Mr. Pepper?" she begged tearfully of the Guard. The tall Rasher looked down at her doubtfully, but Salt, who had hold of Carter, and was just behind, shook his turban violently.

"If we fail to obey the Pasha, we, ourselves, will be thrown to this tiger," sputtered Salt grimly.

"That's right," chimed in Vinegar and Mustard, who were bringing up the procession with the Vegetable Man's cart. "Let's hurry through with it!" And turning a deaf ear to the pleas of the prisoners, the Rash Guardsmen rushed them across the lawn, up the steep steps and threw them over the prison wall. Then, without one backward glance, they marched off to the palace.

Too breathless to run, Betsy picked herself up and looked fearfully around for the tiger. Ugh! There he was and growling frightfully, for the vegetable cart and all the vegetables had hit him on the head. Slashing right and left and shaking himself so violently, that potatoes, beets and apples flew in every direction, he rose and started toward her. This, after all the

other frightful happenings of the morning, was too much and covering her face, Betsy burst into tears. But if Betsy was frightened, the Hungry Tiger was perfectly petrified.

"Betsy! Betsy!" panted the astonished beast. "How in Oz did you get here?" And rubbing his soft nose against her cheek, he began to dry her tears with his tongue. At the first sound of that familiar voice, Betsy's eyes flew open and next instant she had both arms round the Hungry Tiger's neck, hugging him for dear life.

"Carter! Carter!" called the little girl excitedly, "Don't be scared. It's the Hungry Tiger, the Hungry Tiger of Oz!" She fairly sang out the name, in her relief and happiness. The Vegetable Man had dropped head first into the tiger's tub of water. At Betsy's cries, he made a valiant attempt to rise, but when he saw her actually embracing the tiger he was so startled and horrified that he fell back with a splash.

"Hungry Tiger!" gurgled Carter, bobbing up and down like a cork, "Hungry Tiger! Then so much the worse for us!"

CHAPTER 6
The Scarlet Prince

"WOULD you mind not using my drinking cup for a bath," observed the Hungry Tiger mildly, as Carter continued to gurgle and splash about in the tub. Laughing with relief, Betsy seized the Vegetable Man's hands and pulled him out of the water.

"Don't be scared," whispered Betsy comfortably. "This tiger's a friend of mine and he wouldn't hurt anybody!"

"Then what's he doing here?" asked Carter accusingly. "Is this parsnippy Pasha his friend, too?" The Hungry Tiger winced guiltily at Betsy's kind little speech, but resolved that she

58

should never know he had willingly come to Rash.

"I'm his prisoner," he explained in a hollow voice. (And, indeed, he was terribly hollow by this time.) "I'm a prisoner like yourselves." In a husky roar, he told of his trip by hurry-cane to Irashi's Kingdom and of his imprisonment in the Rash courtyard.

"So this light fingered Ippty brought you here," mused Carter wonderingly. "But why?"

"To eat the Rash Prisoners," answered the Hungry Tiger faintly.

"And have you eaten any?" Betsy regarded her old friend anxiously.

"Well, not yet," admitted the Hungry Tiger, rolling his eyes mournfully at the little girl. "Not yet!"

"Have a cabbage," quavered Carter, waving toward the overturned vegetable cart. "Have a cauliflower or a nice bunch of beets." The Hungry Tiger was a perfect stranger to him, and Carter could not feel the same confidence in the beast that Betsy seemed to feel.

"More vegetables," groaned the tiger, sniffing the air sadly. "Well, I suppose they are better than nothing. But tell me Betsy, how in Oz did you ever get here and who," he blinked rapidly at the strange figure of Carter Green, "who is this person?"

With a little chuckle, Betsy introduced the Vegetable Man, then as quickly as she could told of their amazing adventures with the winding road and quick sandals and of Carter's unfortunate experience in the Pasha's garden.

"Isn't there some way out of here?" asked the little girl, looking around nervously. "Oh! What's that?" A dismal wail, issuing from the stones beneath her feet, made Betsy leap into the air.

"It's that singer again," growled the Hungry Tiger and, lashing his tail a little, he put his nose close to the crevice in the blocks. "Less noise down there," he roared warningly.

"I always sing when I'm hungry," answered the singer. "Oh, I'm so hungry!"

"Hand me a tomato or something," rumbled the Hungry Tiger. "Quick!" The Vegetable Man made haste to obey, bringing several tomatoes and a dozen apples as well. Looking up at the wall to see that he was not observed, the Hungry Tiger pushed them hurriedly through the crevice. As the last apple disappeared, a moist song, punctuated with sobs, came sighing upward.

"Oh beautiful Tiger, I love you so,
To you, snif snuffle, my life I owe.
And I'll devote it to songs of praise
And sing, snif, snif, to you, all of my days!"

"Mercy!" gasped Betsy Bobbin. The Hungry Tiger was so embarrassed by the sad singer's ditty that, for a few minutes, he couldn't roar a word. Then, as Carter and Betsy continued to look at him inquiringly, he explained how he had hidden the Rash Singer instead of eating him.

"See!" cried Betsy, turning proudly to the Vegetable Man. "I told you he wouldn't hurt anyone! I think you're just the dearest splendidest tiger I ever—."

"Sh!" cautioned the Hungry Tiger. "Here comes another prisoner. Quick, now, pretend you're afraid of me!" Betsy and the Vegetable Man had just time to crouch back against the wall, when the guards dropped another Rasher into the courtyard.

"It's a barber," whispered Betsy, in an interested voice, and she was right, for clutched in one hand the prisoner had a mug full of suds and in the other a gleaming razor.

"What frightful luck," moaned the Hungry Tiger. "If it had only been a bandit or a robber I could have eaten him without a qualm, but a barber, ugh, he smells of bay rum. Stop that racket, fellow, and let me think!"

And certainly, the poor tiger had plenty to occupy his thoughts, for if things went on in this fashion the underground cavern would soon be full and then what would happen? And how ever was he to get little Betsy Bobbin safely back to Oz? Paying no attention to the terrified squeals of the barber, the Hungry Tiger began to pace restlessly up and down the courtyard, till Betsy, feeling sorry for the frightened little man, ran out and assured him he was in no danger of being eaten.

It was a long time before the barber stopped shivering, but at last, thoroughly convinced, he hurried impetuously after the tiger. "Let me trim your beautiful whiskers," he begged tremulously.

"Trim mine," invited Carter, as the Hungry Tiger impatiently shook his head. The Vegetable Man's rootlike beard had sprouted a foot since morning, so, trembling with relief and gratitude, the Rash barber stood upon the edge of the tub and trimmed it most skillfully, trying at the same time to bring Carter's celery top hair into some kind of order. When the Vegetable Man, in answer to the barber's questions, had told a bit about himself and Betsy, the barber related how he had accidently cut the cheek of Irashi, while shaving him.

"Just a tiny scratch," explained the barber, "and for that I was condemned to die."

"But why do you have such a bad King?" exclaimed Betsy, impatiently. "Why don't you put him out and elect another?"

"We've tried," sighed the barber dolefully, "but Irashi has the army in his power, and with Ippty's help has outwitted us every time."

"Is Ippty the fellow with the fountain pen finger?" asked Betsy curiously.

The barber nodded. "He has a handful of odd fingers," he continued despondently, "a pencil, a sealing wax finger, an eraser, a candle thumb and a pen-knife besides. Oh, he's a

62

handy rogue for a fellow like Irashi, but the real ruler of Rash is Asha, the brother of the present Pasha. Weary of the cares of state, he retired to an unknown country to study radio, leaving his small son and Fizzenpop to govern the Kingdom. No sooner had he gone than Irashi seized the throne and hid the little Prince away. Until we find the lost Prince, nothing can be done," finished the Rash Barber sorrowfully.

"Well, I'll tell Ozma on him," declared Betsy determinedly, "just as soon as I get back to the Emerald City."

"Do you think we ever *will* get back?" The Hungry Tiger paused in his restless walk and regarded the little group mournfully. "I've been here two days and there's not a chink anywhere in this wall."

"Let's all look," proposed Betsy, jumping up, and encouraged by her cheerfulness, the four prisoners made a careeful tour of the pink courtyard. But after several hours had been spent in an unsuccessful search, even Betsy grew downhearted.

"Shall we have something to eat?" asked the little girl, as they all dropped down wearily beside the Hungry Tiger's water tub. "It's a good thing they threw that cart over. At least, we won't starve!" Insisting that this was his part of the performance, Carter passed round tomatoes and apples, till everyone felt refreshed.

Even the Hungry Tiger, after swallowing several dozen of each, admitted that he felt a little less hollow.

"Make the most of the day time," advised the Hungry Tiger gloomily, "for to-night you are supposed to be eaten and will have to hide down below till we find some way out of Rash!" It was not a pleasant prospect, and though Carter did what he could to keep things cheerful, Betsy and the barber grew quieter and quieter as the afternoon advanced.

No more prisoners were flung over the wall, and as the first stars twinkled out, the three slipped silently into the underground cave. The Hungry Tiger had just pushed the pink paving stone back, when Irashi and Ippty, preceded by the pink Guards bearing torches, stepped out upon the wall.

"Good evening, furious feline!" called Ippty shrilly. "How do you do and how do you do it? He's eaten the entire lot," he explained in a breathless whisper to Irashi.

"We've brought you some dessert," announced the Pasha, who seemed to be in a high good humor. "A tempting little waif. Throw the little waif over," he called playfully to the Guards. The Hungry Tiger had immediately turned his back upon these Rash rascals, but as a crumpled little bundle came tumbling down beside him, he swung around. What he saw made him roar so ferociously that Irashi, Ippty and the pink Guards covered their ears and fled from the wall.

"What's he saying?" gasped the Pasha, sinking down on a pink settee and clapping his fat hands to his quivering middle.

"He's talking tiger, your Highness," stuttered Ippty, with a slight shudder, "and tiger is a language I never studied. But never mind, from now on, we are the sole rulers of Rash!" Thumping the Pasha upon the back, Ippty led him into the throne room. As soon as they had gone, the Hungry Tiger stopped roaring and gently approached the small prisoner.

"Don't cry," begged the Hungry Tiger miserably. It was dreadful to have everyone afraid of him, especially a helpless little boy. "Why, he's no older than Betsy," thought the Hungry Tiger, bristling with anger at Irashi's wickedness. "If you stop crying, I'll take you for a

ride all round the courtyard," he promised breathlessly. This offer so astonished the little fellow that he took his arm from before his face and blinked through his tears at the huge beast. There was no mistaking the kindly expression in the Hungry Tiger's eyes, and with a gasp of relief he jumped up and was about to mount the great beast, when a thin figure leapt from the top of the wall and came hurtling down between them.

"Spare him! Spare him, cruel monster!" wheezed the newcomer hoarsely. "I am old and thin, but eat me instead." Placing himself between the Hungry Tiger and the boy, the old Rasher extended his arms pleadingly. It was Fizzenpop, and as the Hungry Tiger drew back with embarrassment and surprise, the Grand Vizier of Rash flung himself at his feet.

"It is the Scarlet Prince!" panted Fizzenpop, beating his head up and down upon the stones, "Prince Evered of Rash!"

"Sh—!" warned the Hungry Tiger, looking about uneasily. Then as Fizzenpop continued his entreaties, he held up his paw for silence. "You're a nice old bone," sighed the Hungry Tiger. "But even so, I have no desire to eat you. It's my conscience," he continued heavily. "I've lived among people too long to hold a position like this." The Grand Vizier could scarcely believe his ears.

"But the other prisoners?" he demanded wildly. "You have eaten them?" The Hungry Tiger, with a tired shake of his head, waved toward the loosened paving stone. The two corn ears of the Vegetable Man were sticking up through the crevice and he was carefully repeating to those below everything as it happened.

"How can I ever thank you!" exclaimed Fizzenpop, prostrating himself again at the Hungry Tiger's feet.

"Don't thank me, help me," begged the Hungry Tiger uncomfortably. "And tell me more about this little chap. Perhaps together we can plan a way to escape." Fizzenpop's brave action in offering himself in place of the little Prince made the Hungry Tiger feel terribly ashamed. More and more he was coming to realize that he would never be able to devour a live man. It was a long story, and sitting down

beside the water tub with Prince Evered in his lap, the Grand Vizier told how Irashi had stolen the throne of the Kingdom and made himself Pasha of Rash.

"There are three magic rubies to protect the rightful rulers of Rash," explained Fizzenpop in a low voice. "One protects him from all danger by water, one protects him from all injury in the air and the other from all harm on the earth or under the earth. The rubies are embedded among other gems in the Rash scepter. No sooner had Evered's father retired than Irashi began to scheme and plan to make himself king. Knowing he could do nothing while the Rash rubies were in our possession, he managed, with Ippty's help, to steal the royal scepter. Next he had the little Prince seized and hidden away. After searching in vain for many months, I chanced yesterday into a Rash Cobbler's shop and found Evered playing with the cobbler's children. Hoping to get him safely out of the country I hurried him back to the palace, but Irashi soon discovered him and the rest," Fizzenpop groaned heavily, "the rest, you know!"

"But what became of the rubies?" asked the Hungry Tiger, as Fizzenpop continued to stroke the head of the little Prince. So much had happened in the last few hours that even Fizzenpop's story could not keep the Prince awake.

"One he hurled from the highest turret of the palace, another he flung into the Rash River and the last he buried somewhere in the garden," answered the Grand Vizier sadly. "Until we recover the three magic rubies the Prince's very life is in danger and Rash must remain under the wicked rule of Irashi, the Rough. Every evening, when I am unobserved, I have searched most diligently for these precious gems, but without any success."

"Well, Irashi won't rule long if I can find a way out of here," growled the Hungry Tiger. "Think, man! Is there no way out?" Fizzenpop shook his head dejectedly and then, as it was growing late, they thought it best to conceal the little Prince with the rest of the prisoners.

"Betsy," called the Hungry Tiger softly. There was no answer and, pulling aside the pink paving block, he peered down into the cavern. "They must be asleep," muttered the

Hungry Tiger in surprise. "Here, Mr. Fizzen-pop, you keep watch while I lower the boy." It was too dark to see, and after the Hungry Tiger had eased the ragged little Prince into the cave, he decided to step in himself and see how everything was going. So he slipped gently down into the darkness.

For nearly ten minutes Fizzenpop kept an anxious eye upon the wall. Then, feeling he had given the Hungry Tiger ample time to replace the block, he turned round. There was no one in the courtyard.

"Merciful mustard!" gasped the Grand Vizier, dashing over to the opening. Hanging down by his heels, he glared into the damp little chamber. But it was perfectly empty. No tiger! No Prince! No barber! No anything! Falling in, head first, Fizzenpop began feeling all over the walls and floors. Then, as his search yielded nothing, he raised his voice in a long dismal wail.

"What's wrong?" Three Rash Guards appeared sleepily on the wall and presently Irashi, himself, wrapped in a pink bath robe, rushed out to see what was the matter.

"The Tiger!" gulped Fizzenpop wildly, "the Hungry Tiger has escaped!" Fizzenpop was already in great disfavor, owing to his discovery of the lost Prince, and realizing instantly that it would never do to tell Irashi the whole truth he resolved to save himself for his country and Evered by a clever story. So, while Irashi listened breathlessly from the wall, he told how he had come out to observe the great creature from Oz, how he had seen him prying up a paving stone and had sprung into the courtyard to prevent him from escaping. "But I was too late!" lamented Fizzenpop shaking his head mournfully. "The Hungry Tiger has disappeared by some miracle of magic!"

"And such a useful beast," sniffed Irashi. "But you shall be rewarded Fizzenpop, for this brave action," and ordering the Guards to let down ropes to the Grand Vizier, the Pasha of Rash went regretfully back to bed. "Oh, well," he yawned as he dropped into a doze, "he's eaten that pest of a Prince and that is something."

CHAPTER 7
Escape from Rash

AFTER the Hungry Tiger had pushed back the pink block, Betsy and her two companions settled themselves as comfortably as they could in the little cavern. It was too dark to see, but they could hear the sad singer crooning drearily to himself. Carter immediately ran his fingers along the floor. Fortunately it was stone.

"No danger of taking root here," he whispered in a relieved voice to Betsy. "Hello, what's that racket?" That racket, as we already know, was Irashi and the pink Guardsmen, and as the noise continued, the Vegetable Man, who was tallest, stuck his ears through the crevice between the blocks. What Carter heard through his corn ears was simply amazing, and as he immediately repeated it to the little company below, they soon forgot their discomfort in their interest. When Fizzenpop explained who the last prisoner was, the barber threw his shaving mug joyfully into the air and began to prance wildly up and down upon the shins of the sad singer.

"Three cheers for the Scarlet Prince!" roared the barber, thumping on the wall with his razor. "Three cheers for Prince Evered of Rash!"

"Be quiet," begged Betsy anxiously, "they'll hear you. Oh, hush!" But the barber refused to be restrained and continued to thump enthusiastically upon the wall. Withdrawing his ears from the crevice, Carter groped about in the dark in an effort to stop the reckless fellow, but at the third snatch, the whole side of the cavern fell away and pitched the entire company into a dark damp tunnel. Carter managed to slip his arm round Betsy Bobbin, as he fell past her, and they could hear the sputter and groans of the Rash barber and the singer far below. "Anyway!" gasped Betsy, as they skidded down the slippery passageway together, "anyway we're out of Rash!"

"Is this anyway," groaned the Vegetable Man, trying to keep himself and Betsy right side up. "Well, if this is anyway, I prefer some other way. Whew!"

Betsy was about to reply when the floor of the tunnel dropped out and they fell straight downward, then, striking a rubbery incline, shot straight upward. The rest of the trip was more like a rush through a scenic railway tunnel than anything Betsy ever had experienced. Up slides, down slides, round loops, bends and curves, swooped the Rash prisoners till there was no breath left in any one of them. And when, after a half hour of it, they shot out into the open, they lay for nearly five minutes, perfectly motionless, where they had fallen. Then the Rash singer sat up and in a strangled voice quavered:

> "We're down! We're down and out of Rash,
> And everything has gone to smash!
> Snif! Snif! A trip like this upsets me,
> But how we got here is what gets me!"

Probably he would have continued his song indefinitely, but at that minute all of Carter's vegetables, which had slid more slowly down the tunnel, sprayed out of the opening and simply overwhelmed him. Betsy had not breath enough to laugh, but Carter, not being so easily winded, sprang up and ran to the singer's assistance.

"They always throw things when I sing," sobbed the poor fellow, as Carter helped him to his feet, and a little defiantly he repeated his last stanza:

"Snif! Snif! A trip like this upsets me,
But how we got here is what gets me!"

"It gets me, too," mumbled the barber, rolling over and looking around for his razor. "One minute there we are and next minute there we ain't! Strikes me this ground is pretty soft. Why, it's down," he puffed, blowing a ball of fuzz from the end of his nose.

Betsy, pulling up a handful of what she supposed to be grass, found her fingers full of feathers, for they had landed in the very center of a field of down. "Well, this probably saved us from breaking our heads, but how did it all happen?" repeated the barber, looking over at Carter in perfect bewilderment.

"It was your fault," answered the Vegetable Man gravely. "You must have touched some secret spring when you pounded on the wall. I don't know whether to thank you or not," sighed Carter rubbing his thin ankles doubtfully.

"I hope you didn't bark your shins on the tunnel," murmured the barber solicitously.

"No," answered Carter frankly, "I didn't bark my shins for they are bark already, but you've ruined my business." He looked ruefully at his scattered vegetables. They had not stood the trip at all well and were lying about in squashed heaps.

"Never mind, Buddy!" The barber clapped Carter comfortably on the back. "Maybe you can pick up some more down here. But where is here, I wonder?"

"Well, any place is better than Rash," exclaimed Betsy, looking about curiously. "The last time I fell through a tunnel I went clear to the other side of the world. Do you s'pose this is the other side of the world? Look, there's the moon!"

"It's square!" whispered the sad singer in a frightened voice. "And it's green!" he added dismally.

> "The moon, the moon, the moon is there,
> But never trust a moon that's square!
> It's shining squarely on our heads;
> We'll all be slaughtered in our beds!"

"You don't know what you're singing about," declared the barber gruffly. "A square moon is better than no moon and there aren't any beds that I can see, but there's a town over yonder. Look!" Not far away, shadowy and mysterious in the green light of the square moon, rose the towers and spires of a strange city.

"Well, I wish the Hungry Tiger were here," cried Betsy Bobbin. "And the little Prince. I wonder if the cave wall closed up after it slid us down here?"

Whiz! Whirr! Bang! As if in answer to Betsy's question, the two came sailing out of the tunnel, circled through the air and landed close beside Betsy. And while the Hungry Tiger was still puffing and panting with indignation and surprise, the little girl flung her arms about his neck and told him the whole story of their flight through the mysterious passageway. Slowly the big beast got his breath back and as he blew the downy feathers from his nose, the Rash Barber, with great ceremony, introduced the little Prince to Betsy Bobbin. In the green moonlight she saw a pleasant, freckle-faced little boy of about her own age. His nose turned up, his collar turned down, and in spite of his ragged clothes he had a most kingly bearing. Betsy knew at once that they would be friends. Prince Evered, himself, liked the little girl immediately and after they had compared notes on their terrible fall, he begged her to tell him more about the Vegetable Man.

"Is he really real?" asked the little Prince, scarcely taking his eyes from Carter's curious figure. Betsy nodded and told him all about her meeting with the Vegetable Man, her trip across the Deadly Desert and of their arrival in Rash. She was going on to tell him little about Ozma and the Emerald City, but the sad singer had started such a sleepy song of welcome to honor the little Prince that she could not keep her eyes open. Evered, too, soon began to nod and as the Hungry Tiger had wisely determined not to investigate the strange city till morning, they all curled up in the fields of down and were soon fast asleep. All but Carter Green. Since turning to a vegetable he did not require rest and all night long he paced up and down the white feathery field, thinking his own queer thoughts and keeping a loving watch over his new and interesting friends.

CHAPTER 8

In Down Town

WHEN Betsy awakened next morning, she saw the Hungry Tiger and Carter staring curiously at a huge sign in the corner of the field.

"Down!" ordered the sign sternly, "No Uppers Allowed!"

"That means us, I suppose," said Carter, scratching his corn ear reflectively. "I wonder what kind of people live down here?"

"Geese!" spluttered the Hungry Tiger, looking cross-eyed at a fluff of feathers that had lighted on the end of his nose. "Wish I could catch a couple, I'm *so* hungry!"

"So am I," agreed Betsy, "and I don't see a thing to eat, do you?"

"Nothing but sun-beams," mused Carter, "and they'd make a pretty little breakfast, but we ought to be glad there's a sun so far underground."

"Why, shouldn't there be?" snapped the Hungry Tiger. Being hungry made him a bit irritable. "Doesn't the sun go down every day?" Betsy and Carter exchanged startled glances, for neither of them had thought of this; and the little girl, gazing dreamily across the soft fields, began to wonder what exciting adventures and strange experiences lay ahead of them. But the Hungry Tiger was more interested in food. "Maybe there'll be something to eat in the city," he wheezed in a weak voice. "Let's waken the others." Prince Evered and the sad singer were already up and after a few shakes and thumps on the back, the Rash Barber lifted his head.

"What's up?" he inquired sleepily.

"Nothing," giggled Betsy. "Don't you remember we all fell down?"

"Don't remember a thing since I hit the feathers," yawned the barber, plucking a tuft of down from his beard.

"Well, this is Down," laughed Betsy, pointing to the sign.

"And time to get up," added the Hungry Tiger gruffly. "We're going off to that city over there to see if we can find some breakfast.

Jump on my back Betsy, and you, too." The
Hungry Tiger nodded at the ragged little Prince.
"What do they call you?"

"The Scarlet Prince, the Son of Asha,
Prince Evered of Rash, the Pasha!"

Droned the sad singer with a deep salaam
toward the youthful huler.

"All that?" gasped the Hungry Tiger, putting
back his ears.

"Oh, call me 'Reddy'," exclaimed the little
boy, hopping up behind Betsy. "I haven't been
Prince for a year, you know, and that's what
Fizzenpop called me even when I was."

"Well, I wish Fizzenpop were here now,"
sighed the Hungry Tiger regretfully, "too bad
the trap door closed before he found it." The
tiger had a great admiration for the Grand
Vizier of Rash and determined to do all in his
power to restore Reddy to his throne.

"Tell us more about the magic rubies,"
begged Betsy, as the tiger started briskly across
the fields of Down.

"Yes, do," urged the Vegetable Man, "we
dropped out right in the middle of the story
and most of it was knocked out of my head."
Carter was trudging along beside the Hungry
Tiger, but the barber and the singer, thinking
it presumptuous to walk so close to the Prince,
had dropped respectfully behind. So while the
strange little procession moved toward the

unknown city, Prince Evered told again how Irashi had stolen the precious rubies and made himself Pasha of Rash.

"Well, I don't see how you'll ever find them," murmured Betsy, when he had finished the story and told a little of his life with the cobbler's children.

"Nothing's impossible," Carter reminded her gaily. "Look at me!" Betsy and the little Prince both had to grin, for the Vegetable Man did look impossible, and yet, there he was.

"But how would you know the rubies if you did find them?" asked Betsy, after a little pause.

"There is an 'R' cut in each one," explained Reddy gravely, "and they are square."

"R!" shouted Carter, snatching out a stalk of his celery. "R? Parsnips and peonies! Radishes and rhubarb!" Seizing the leather pouch from about his neck, the Vegetable Man dumped its whole contents into Betsy's lap. "Stop!" begged Carter grasping the Hungry Tiger by the tail. "Stop, I think I've discovered something."

"To eat?" questioned the Hungry Tiger, looking round eagerly. Without answering, Carter picked up the ruby he had already showed to Betsy Bobbin.

"Square!" puffed Carter triumphantly, "and it has an R cut on the side!"

"Why, it's one of the Rash Rubies," screamed the Prince, nearly tumbling off the tiger. "Where did you find that?" Passing the beautiful gem from one to the other, Carter explained how he had found it in a potato he had bought from a gypsy.

"But which ruby is it?" panted the barber, pressing forward. "It might be the one Irashi flung from the castle window, or it might be the one he buried in the garden. Let me give your Highness a tiny cut with my razor," he suggested brightly. "Then, if it does not hurt, we will know that it is the ruby that protects you from danger on the earth or under the earth."

Evered looked a little doubtful, and the Hungry Tiger shook his head impatiently. "Too risky," growled the tiger.

"Let his Highness climb yonder tree," proposed the singer, waving toward a feather fan tree that stood not far away. "Then let him fall out. If he breaks no bones we will know it is the ruby that protects him from danger in the air."

"Don't you do it!" cried Betsy indignantly. "It might be the ruby that protects you from danger in the water. Then where'd you be?"

"Let Reddy keep his ruby till danger threatens," advised the Hungry Tiger sternly. "I'm not going to have him sliced and broken if I can help it." And he flashed his yellow eyes so threateningly that the barber and singer fell back in confusion.

"But wasn't it lucky we met Carter!" exclaimed Betsy, as the Vegetable Man slipped the ruby into Evered's pocket. "And if the King of Down lives in this city, and can just show us the way up, maybe we can find the other rubies and—"

"Something to eat," roared the Hungry Tiger, breaking into a quick step.

"When I'm the Pasha, you shall have anything you wish," promised the little Prince, smiling sideways at Carter Green. "You can be Keeper of Kites and Marbles if you want, Betsy shall be Queen, and the Hungry Tiger all the rest of the nobility."

"Thanks," muttered the Hungry Tiger, grinning behind his whiskers. He knew that if he ever reached Oz in safety, nothing could tempt him away from the Emerald City again, not even his terrible appetite.

"But what do the three R's stand for?" asked Carter. He had been turning the matter over in his mind for some time.

"Readin', ritin', and rithmetic," guessed Betsy Bobbin.

"Rightful Ruler of Rash," corrected Reddy, with a cheerful bounce. Now that one of the magic rubies was in his possession anything seemed possible. "Hurry up!" he called over his shoulder to the Rash barber and singer. "We're almost there." And they almost were, for beyond a thin fringe of feather brush rose the high buildings and towers of the city they had seen in the moonlight. The trip across the fields of Down had been rather tiresome. The feet of the travellers sank at each step into the soft feathers, so that even the Hungry Tiger was panting a little when they reached the city itself. Over the gates, creaking backward and forward in the brisk morning breeze, was a large silver sign.

"Down Town," read Betsy, squinting a little in the bright sunshine. "Why, it looks just like down town at home, Carter."

"Home in Oz?" queried the Vegetable Man, pressing his nose against the bars.

"No, in Oklahoma!" laughed Betsy hastily. "But let's go in. I see stores and hotels and everything!"

"Hotels?" gulped the Hungry Tiger, pricking up his ears. "Hotels! B-r-r-r!" And before Betsy or anyone else could stop him, he had hurled himself headlong at the gates of Down Town. With a creak and bang, they burst open and the whole Rash company fell through.

"Food!" roared the Hungry Tiger, charging at full speed down the main street. "Give us food!" At the tiger's roars, such citizens as were in the streets stopped in horror and astonishment. Then, right and left like startled hares, they darted, huddling into doorways, scurrying into side alleys, tumbling over one another in their frenzy to get away. In fact they were as amazed and terrified to see a tiger in their Down Town, as we would be to see one in ours, and when they glimpsed Carter Green, they ran faster than ever.

"Stop!" shouted Betsy, flinging both arms around the tiger's neck to keep from falling off. "You're scaring everyone away. Stop! Here's a restaurant!"

But the Hungry Tiger had already seen the tempting display of pies and roast turkey in the window. Turning so sharply that the Prince of Rash tumbled off backward, he rushed through the swinging doors and next minute they had the establishment to themselves. One look at the Hungry Tiger had been enough for the early morning customers. Grabbing their hats, and without waiting for their change, they pelted out the rear door of the shop, followed by three waiters and the screaming proprietor.

"Oh, well," sighed Betsy, helping herself capably to a spring chicken that was turning slowly on a spit, "if they won't stay to wait on us, we must just help ourselves."

"What fun!" chuckled Reddy, burying his

nose in a cherry tart, while the barber and sad singer divided a huge sausage between them. The Vegetable Man, not requiring food, busied himself with counting the oranges and apples in the window and wondered wistfully whether he could not find a cart somewhere and stir up some trade.

But it was the Hungry Tiger who enjoyed himself most of all. At one side of the room a dozen roasts were waiting their turn at the ovens. These, the famished tiger snapped up in so many bites. After his long fast in Rash, they tasted perfectly delicious and, while Reddy looked at him in astonishment and admiration, he swallowed three roast turkeys, a bowl of potato salad and a tray full of biscuits. He was just starting on a huge ham, when a commotion in the doorway made them all spin round. It was the proprietor, and with him were twenty tall officers.

They had a great net, and as the Hungry Tiger gave a convulsive swallow, they flung it over him and dragged the huge beast, the singer, the barber, Betsy, the Vegetable Man, and the little Prince of Rash out into the street.

"Robbers!" screamed the proprietor savagely, as they were hustled away. "Wait till Dad hears of this."

"Why don't you bite them?" wailed Betsy, trying to wriggle out of the grasp of the officer who had her by the arm.

"Too full," mumbled the Hungry Tiger in a stuffy voice. "Couldn't eat another bite, not even a policeman. But it was worth it and who's afraid of Dad? We've been arrested before and gotten away. We'll get off somehow, trust me."

"Maybe the ruby will help," said the little Prince, squirming about so he could see Betsy. Carter, on the other side, gave her such an encouraging wink that the little girl stopped worrying and began to look around with real interest. Down Town, as Betsy had said in the first place, was quite like other down towns, except that there were no motors nor wagons and the men who crowded the streets were gaily costumed in green and yellow bills. Four of the Down Officers had hold of the net entangling the Hungry Tiger, one officer had

88

hold of each of the others and the rest tramped importantly ahead of the procession.

"Who's Dad?" asked Betsy, as they were propelled through the swinging doors of a large white bank.

"The King," answered the officer haughtily.

"Is he a kind King?" sniffed the sad singer nervously. "What kind of a King is Dad. Will he make us happy or make us sad?"

"You'll soon see," grunted the officer, pushing him roughly into an elevator. The others were thrust as unceremoniously after him, the car shot upward and the next minute they were all marched out upon the roof. In a swivel chair on top of the bank, sat Dad. He was reading a paper and beside him on a high stool sat the most curious lady Betsy had ever seen.

"Their Majesties the King and Queen of Down Town!" boomed the officer, who had hold of Betsy Bobbin. "Robbers, your Highness!" he announced with a low bow.

CHAPTER 9
The Indus Tree

A T the officer's ringing words, King Dad lowered his paper, and as he got a good look at the Hungry Tiger, his chair fell forward with a crash.

"A tiger, Nance!" stuttered Dad, rolling his eyes wildly at the Queen.

"But it's tied," answered the Queen of Down Town calmly. "What are the charges officer?"

"Ninety-nine dollars and sixty-eight cents," answered the officer hoarsely, and leaning over he handed Dad a long slip of paper.

"But we only wanted a little breakfast," began Betsy tremulously, "and——"

"A little breakfast!" wheezed Dad, and putting on his specs started to read off the list:

"Twelve roasts,
Four turkeys,
One spring chicken,
Three dozen tarts,
Fourteen doughnuts
One ham and twenty-four biscuits,
Three quarts of potato salad,
One six-pound sausage."

"Monstrous!" muttered the Queen, tapping her foot indignantly on the floor. "They shall pay well for this."

"Why, that's a mere bite for a fellow like me," rumbled the Hungry Tiger, impatiently, "and I ate most of it."

"Who—who are you?" demanded Dad, holding on to the arms of his chair and blinking nervously at the great beast.

"I am the Hungry Tiger of Oz, and these are my friends. We are on our way to the Emerald City. This little girl is Betsy Bobbin and allow me to present the Vegetable Man and the Pasha of—"

"Your tale drags," yawned her Majesty, fanning herself with her handkerchief. "Cut it short. Time is money down here and the thing for you to do is to pay up and settle down."

"How clearly you put things," murmured Dad, looking affectionately at his Queen. Betsy had been staring at Her Highness in perfect

astonishment, for she was made entirely of money. Her face and hair were of purest gold, her hands and feet of silver and her dress was made from hundreds of yellow bills that crinkled crisply when she moved. Yet, with all her glitter and brilliance, she seemed to Betsy the hardest and most disagreeable being she had ever met. Dad himself looked kind and care-worn, resembling vaguely many of the daddies Betsy had known in the United States. If he had just decided things for himself and not depended so much upon the Queen, Betsy would have liked him better.

"Well, are you ready to pay up?" asked Dad, looking from one to the other of the travellers. "Ninety-nine dollars and sixty-eight cents, please."

"But we haven't any money," explained Betsy

breathlessly. "We started off in such a hurry and—"

"You should not have come Down Town if you had no money," muttered Dad reprovingly.

"How dare you be without money?" cried the Queen, springing up in a perfect fury. "How dare you come Down Town without money?"

"Now, don't get frenzied, Fi Nance," begged Dad, patting her anxiously on the hand. "They can easily make some money, you know." His words seemed to soothe the Queen.

"That's so," she mused thoughtfully. "Anybody can make money Down Town, if they just try hard enough." Almost pleasantly she turned to Betsy. "You, my child," purred the Queen, resuming her seat, "you, may start as a cash girl. I myself was a cash girl once," she went on dreamily, "and now look at me—Fi Nance, Queen of Down Town. I'm simply made of money!"

Betsy looked, and shuddered a little as she did so. She was about to tell the Queen that she had no desire to be a cash girl, when Fi Nance haughtily held up her hand for silence. "The lad shall be an office boy," she decided imperiously. "Who did you say he was?"

"A Prince," growled the Hungry Tiger.

"A dry goods store will be the best place for him," murmured Dad. "What can you two do?" he demanded, looking over his specs at the barber and sad singer of Rash.

"Anything! Anything!" whined the frightened

prisoners, bumping their heads together in their anxiety to please.

"Pooh!" sniffed Dad scornfully. "That means nothing whatsoever."

"Shampoo?" suggested the barber hopefully. "Let me give your Highness a little shave and hair cut."

"Are you a barber?" asked Dad, looking at the Rasher with more interest. "If you're a barber, you can stay and welcome. There's always room for another barber, Down Town."

"Thank you! Thank you! If your majesty will permit—" The barber bowed apologetically to the Prince of Rash, "I will remain here. I have always wanted to make money," he acknowledged frankly.

"Me too!" gulped the sad singer eagerly.

"I've sung until I'm hoarse, in Rash,
And never earned a cent in cash!"

"He has a voice like a horse," whispered Dad, in a loud aside to the Queen.

"He sings like a jack-ass!" agreed Her Majesty readily. "But let him stay. Any kind of a noise goes, Down Town. Now as to these others?" She rolled her golden eyes in perplexity and disapproval at the Vegetable Man and the Hungry Tiger; then evidently giving them up, cried in a loud voice, "The audience is over and the prisoners are discharged. Let them make some money, pay up and settle down."

The Indus Tree

"Well, goodbye!" smiled Dad, picking up his paper with a sigh of relief. "If you don't like the positions we have chosen for you, go down to the square and choose some others. Take them to the public square!" he ordered, waving at the officers.

So, much to Betsy's and the little Prince's amusement, they were all hurried into the elevator, out of the bank and marched along the streets of the city. A curious sign on the first corner puzzled Betsy very much.

"Down Town belongs to the Daddies," said the sign severely, "No aunts, mothers or sisters allowed."

"Why, anybody can go down town at home," exclaimed the little girl in surprise.

"I noticed there were no ladies about,"

observed Carter in an amused voice. "The Daddies have it all their own way here."

As they passed along, Betsy looked curiously in the windows of the shops and offices and saw that everywhere the Dads were making money. Some were making money out of leather, some were making money out of oil and some were even making money out of old papers and rags. It looked quite simple.

"But there must be some trick to it," she whispered hurriedly to the Prince of Rash. "I hope we don't have to stay here long. I won't be a cash girl."

Prince Evered nodded emphatically, for he had no intention of becoming an office boy. Just then they came to the public square and were marched solemnly through the gates.

"Pick your tools and get started," ordered the first officer gruffly, and grumbling a little among themselves, because the prisoners had got off so easily, the twenty tall Downsmen tramped noisily back to their station. As soon as they had gone, the barber, with his razor, released the Hungry Tiger from the net.

"I wonder what they meant about tools," murmured Betsy, staring all around her. "Why what an enormous tree!" It stood in the center of the square, spreading out in every direction, its branches weighed down with a most curious collection of objects. There was a small notice tacked on the trunk and Evered and Betsy Bobbin hurried over to investigate.

The Indus Tree

"Indus Tree," read the sign. "Pick your trade, business or profession here."

"Well, I've often heard of the big industries," gasped Carter Green, squinting up through the branches, "but I never knew they looked like this. If we are to stay Down Town, I suppose we had better pick our business at once."

"Stay if you want to," rumbled the Hungry Tiger impatiently. "My business is to see that Betsy Bobbin gets safely back to Oz and to restore Reddy to his throne. I, for my part, am going to leave as soon as I can find an exit."

"Maybe they won't let us," faltered Betsy, looking uneasily over her shoulder. But the Daddies were not paying the slightest attention to the little group in the square and, greatly relieved, they turned back to the Indus Tree.

"Some of these things might prove useful, even if we did not remain here," muttered Carter.

"Why, there's a razor!" shouted the Rash barber in delight, and springing into the air, he snapped it off the lower branch and began to finger it lovingly.

"I'd take that harp, if I could just reach it," sighed the sad singer, looking wistfully aloft.

"I'll pick it for you," offered Prince Evered obligingly, and swinging up into the tree he broke the harp from its stem and dropped it into the singer's arms.

"See anything you want, Betsy?" called the little Prince, and pushing aside a cluster of

paint brushes, he peered down at her expectantly. But with so many things to choose from,
it was hard to decide. There were thimbles and
shears, bottles of ink, hammers, saws, buckets
and mops, brooms and hoes, music rolls, miners'
caps, rolling pins, cook books, compasses and
ship models—everything in fact that a body
would need to work with.

While Reddy was waiting for Betsy to make
up her mind, his curiosity carried him higher
and higher into the branches. Carter, too,
walked round and round the base of the tree,
shaking his head and exclaiming from time to
time with surprise and astonishment. But the
Hungry Tiger had small use for a tree that
produced nothing to eat, nor was he interested
in money or making money. So, while the
others examined the marvelous tree, he began
looking for a way out, and presently was

TAKE SUBWAY
HERE FOR
UP TOWN

rewarded, for in the far corner of the square were steps leading down into what seemed to be a tunnel. Stretching his neck cautiously about the doorway, the Hungry Tiger spied some directions.

"Take the subway here for Up Town," said a sign.

"Here! Here! I've found a way out!" roared the Hungry Tiger joyfully.

"What kind of a way?" cried Carter, stumbling over the wheel-barrow he had just plucked from the Indus Tree.

"A subway!" puffed the tiger. "Tell the rest of 'em, quick!"

"Come on! Come on!" cried Carter waving to the others. "The Hungry Tiger has found some way out."

"I said, 'subway!' " growled the tiger a bit temperishly. "Are you going to take that thing along with you?" The Vegetable Man looked lovingly at the wheel-barrow.

"It was the nearest thing to a cart I could find," he murmured sadly, "and will come in very handy if I pick up some vegetables or fruit. So will this." He patted a small spade that had grown on the same branch with the wheel-barrow. "Hello, here they come now!" At Carter's cries, the little Prince of Rash, who had been trying to decide between a policeman's club and a sword, plucked the sword and came crashing to earth, followed by several bottles of ink and an ironing board.

"I may have to fight for my Kingdom," he told Betsy importantly, "and this sword will help." Betsy nodded understandingly, and without waiting to pick anything for herself she ran over to the Hungry Tiger. They were all anxious to leave Down Town, and when Betsy told them a little about subways (she had often been in subways in the United States) the Hungry Tiger gave the signal to start.

"We've fogotten the barber and the singer," exclaimed Betsy, pausing suddenly on the top step. But just then the two Rashers came hurrying over, and when the Hungry Tiger announced that they were going Up Town and from there back to the Marvelous Land of Oz, both drew back.

"I've had enough ups and downs in my life," sighed the barber, "and will remain here and make my fortune. By that time Prince Evered may, perchance, be restored to his throne. Then and then only will I return to Rash." The singer, after one look into the gloomy opening, declared that he too, preferred to stay Down Town.

"With this harp and my beautiful voice, I will soon be a rich man," he assured them earnestly, and with many goodbyes and good wishes the four travellers left them to make their fortunes. Long after they had descended the steps and entered the subway itself, they could hear the plaintive wails of the sad singer and the thrum of the harp he had picked from the Indus Tree.

It was dim and mysterious in the underground passageway, and after looking in vain for a car or train to carry them Up Town, Betsy began following the arrows painted on the white washed walls.

"There ought to be a car somewhere," panted the little girl, after they had made at least fifty turns.

"Try mine," invited Carter, and with a tired smile Betsy dropped into the wheel-barrow. Reddy was riding the Hungry Tiger, and after they had proceeded for more than an hour, the arrows stopped altogether.

"Well, this isn't like our subways at all," exclaimed Betsy in disgust. "When you take a subway at home, you get somewhere."

"Isn't this somewhere?" asked Carter, stooping a little so he could enter a rough stone cavern at the end of the tunnel. Whistling cheerfully, he trundled Betsy through the low doorway. The Hungry Tiger followed, sniffing the air suspiciously, and it must be confessed that the little rock chamber did not look very inviting. The walls were of jagged gray stone, the floor damp and slippery and the whole place dismal and chilly as a vault. A feeble light flickered down from an opening in the ceiling and after a discouraged look round, Betsy shook her head.

"We'll have to go back Down Town," she sighed sadly. "I'll have to be a cash girl after all!"

"No you won't!" called Reddy. He had jumped off the tiger and gone to examine the back of the cavern. "Here's a door!" Hurrying over, the others saw that the little Prince was right.

" 'Cave Inn,' " roared the Hungry Tiger, reading the door plate over the little boy's shoulder. " 'Knock three times.' Why, that's fine! If it's an Inn, they'll surely have something to eat. We can't get out so we might as well go in," he finished with a playful wink at Carter. Stepping back a few paces, the Hungry Tiger ran at the door and bumped his head three times against the brass plate. At the third bump, the door of Cave Inn flew open, the floor of the cave itself, tilted forward and the four adventurers fell through. Stones and dirt rattled down after them and the Hungry Tiger's growls mingled with the screams of Betsy and Evered, as they went tumbling down into the darkness.

CHAPTER 10

The Magic Spectacles

KALIKO, King of all the gnomes, and metal monarch besides, sat gloomily on the jewelled rock throne in his underground cavern.

"Nothing ever happens here," complained Kaliko, frowning at his Royal Chamberlain.

"Let's have a war," proposed Guph, looking up from the ruby scepter he was polishing. "We haven't had a war since Ruggedo left."

"Ruggedo!" shrilled Kaliko, stamping his foot furiously. "How dare you mention that name in my presence. Begone! Begone and never speak to me again."

"Then I'll write," mumbled Guph, and picking up his bottle of ruby polish unconcernedly he left the throne room. Ruggedo was the former King and had ruled over the gnomes for many years. He had been deposed for his wickedness by a powerful Jinn and Kaliko was made monarch in his place. Later Ruggedo had tried to capture Oz, itself, and had been banished by Ozma to a lonely isle in the Nonestic Ocean.

But wicked as Ruggedo had been, the gnomes often sighed for his return. Things had been more interesting during Ruggedo's reign and though Kaliko was a good King, he was not half so interesting. Kaliko knew this and any mention of the old gnome king always irritated him intensely. For several moments after Guph's departure, he continued to mutter and mumble with displeasure. Then, suddenly bethinking himself of a new invention of the chief wizard, he reached into his pocket and brought out a green case. In the case was a pair of pink spectacles, not merely spectacles, mind you, but exspectacles, and the gnome wizard had assured the King that with them he could see events before they occurred.

Kaliko had not yet tried this new contrivance, and still grumbling a little he set the exspectacles upon his nose and stared drearily at the rock wall in front of him. He really did not expect anything to happen. Therefore, when four figures appeared suddenly upon the wall, he gave a start of astonishment. Reflected upon the rock surface as clearly as if it were a moving picture, he could see four people making their way through the Lost Labyrinth at the Southern end of his dominions.

"Guph! Guph!" shrieked the Gnome King, pounding vigorously on the gong at his side. "Come back here at once." And when Guph, rather sulkily, appeared, he pointed excitedly at the wall.

"Look! Look!" commanded Kaliko. "It's Betsy Bobbin, the Hungry Tiger of Oz and two others. What in mud is that fellow made of anyway?"

Rubbing his eyes, Guph stared at the wall and then at his master. Then, taking a scrap of paper from a rock desk beside the throne, he scribbled two words on the paper and handed it to the King.

"You're crazy," stated the paper, quite saucily.

"How dare you write to me like that!" fumed Kaliko, tearing the paper in two. "Are you dumb, can't you speak? Are you blind, can't you see?" He waved again at the great rock. Then, suddenly realizing that Guph had not the exspectacles to help him, tore them off and clapped them upon the Chief Chamberlain's nose. Immediately Guph was as excited as Kaliko.

106

"Hurrah!" exulted the little gnome, forgetting his determination not to speak to the King again. "Hurrah! Now we can have a war. Shall I call out the Guard and have the red hot dungeons heated? Hah, Hah, Hah!"

"What are you laughing at?" exclaimed Kaliko, as Guph doubled up with mirth.

"That animated truck garden," panted Guph. "He's fallen on his corn ear and the Hungry Tiger just slipped into a mud hole!"

"Let me see," cried the King, snatching the exspectacles back again. And for the next five minutes Kaliko and his Chief Chamberlain fought bitterly for possession of the magic glasses. As soon as Kaliko had them, Guph wanted to see how the travelers were progressing, and as soon as Guph had them Kaliko insisted on having them back.

"Well, shall we have a war?" grumbled Guph, as Kaliko seized the specs for the seventeenth time.

"Certainly not," answered the King. "Betsy's a good friend of mine. Don't you remember, she was here when Ruggedo was deposed? And I see no harm in these others."

"I thought it would be like this," muttered Guph in disgust. "You're such a goody-goody, you never let us have any fun at all. I suppose you'll end by inviting them all to lunch," he finished bitterly.

"Just what I was thinking of," admitted Kaliko cheerfully. "Pray go and conduct them the rest of the way and don't slam the door when you go out, either." Settling back on his throne with a little chuckle of anticipation, Kaliko continued to watch the progress of Betsy and her friends through the winding corridors of the Lost Labyrinth.

Betsy, herself, did not even know she was in the gnome King's dominions. After a terrible tumble through the dark, the four adventurers had plunged into the underground pool of a grim green grotto. While the water had broken their fall and saved them from serious injury, it had not added to their cheerfulness.

"This is not the ruby that protects me from water," sputtered Prince Evered, as Carter dragged him out of the pool. "Ugh! I'm nearly drowned!"

"Have you still got it?" asked Betsy. The Hungry Tiger had already pulled her out and was helping Carter fish his wheelbarrow from the pool. Feeling in his pocket, the Prince nodded. Then, picking up his sword, he looked around in huge disgust.

"Is this a Cave Inn?" he demanded indignantly.

"I wonder where this passageway leads," murmured Betsy, who had run to an opening in the grotto. "Maybe there's an inn after all." But there was no sign of an inn anywhere—only a maze of rocky corridors branching out in every direction. With Betsy and Reddy on his back, the Hungry Tiger stepped cautiously

out of the grotto and started down the widest of the curious corridors. The floors were slippery with moss covered rocks, the ceiling was of glittering green stones, shaped like long, jagged icicles.

Betsy and the Prince of Rash often had to lie flat on the tiger's back to escape their sharp points, while poor Carter Green was forced to bend double, as he walked. Sure-footed as he was, the Hungry Tiger slipped again and again on the treacherous stones and Carter's progress was a succession of spills, slides and tumbles. Through it all the Vegetable Man maintained his cheerfulness, stubbornly refusing to abandon the wheel-barrow, but after an hour of winding in and out of the dreary labyrinth had still brought them nowhere, even the Vegetable Man grew anxious and sad. A thin blue mold was beginning to form on the end of his nose.

"If I don't get out of here soon, I'll spoil," he wheezed nervously. "Do you see any opening ahead?"

The Hungry Tiger was about to reply when he slipped into the mud-hole that had so amused Guph. This so discouraged the poor beast he said nothing at all. Indeed, the rest of their journey, while interesting to Kaliko, watching comfortably from his throne, was neither interesting or amusing to the travellers themselves. When they came at last to an impassible rock wall and realized they must retrace their steps, Carter sank dejectedly into the wheel-barrow and the Hungry Tiger lay down and

panted with exhaustion. Imagine their astonishment, when a door in the wall suddenly
opened and Guph, bearing a blazing ruby
lantern, appeared before them.

"Follow me," commanded Guph disagreeably.
"His Majesty has foolishly invited you to lunch."

"It's a gnome!" cried Betsy in surprise.
"Why, we must be in the Gnome King's
dominions."

"I was here with Dorothy and Billina, when
we rescued the Queen of Ev and her ten
children," puffed the Hungry Tiger, rising to
his feet. "Ruggedo was King then, but he's
been put out of the Kingdom, I understand."

"I wonder if Kaliko's still King?" exclaimed
Betsy. The little girl had had a whole book of
adventures with Ruggedo and had even been
present at Kaliko's coronation. "Oh, I do hope
Kaliko's the King," she finished earnestly.

111

"Well, if you're going to wonder and hope, stay here," grumbled Guph. "If you're coming to lunch, follow me." Without waiting for an answer, the crooked little elf turned on his heel and started rapidly down the narrow passageway. The Hungry Tiger looked questioningly back at Carter and Carter looked uneasily at Betsy.

"Let's go," decided the little girl sensibly. "If Kaliko's still King I know he'll help us."

"If he don't, I'll slice off his nose," declared Reddy, peering over Betsy's shoulder in an endeavor to catch another glimpse of Guph. He had never seen a gnome before, and as they hurried after the King's messenger, Betsy explained a bit about these queer rock-colored elves, who live under the earth's surface and dig for precious metals and stones. They passed hundreds of the busy little men on their way through the rocky tunnels, and when Guph entered the underground castle of the Gnome King, himself, both Carter Green and Prince Evered gasped with astonishment and admiration. Lighted with jeweled lanterns, spread with silken rugs, furnished with taste and even magnificence, the spacious caverns opened in a blaze of splendor before the visitors. The Gnome King's dwelling was an old story to Betsy and the Hungry Tiger. They were more interested in knowing who was King, and when the tiger, hurrying after Guph, burst suddenly into the throne room, Betsy gave a cry of real pleasure.

"Why, hello, Kaliko!" cried the little girl, jumping down and running over to him eagerly.

"King Kaliko, if you don't mind," whispered the gnome looking nervously at Guph, who was making faces at the Hungry Tiger. "How did you happen into these parts, my dear?"

"We caved in," growled the Hungry Tiger, sniffing the air anxiously. "Is lunch nearly ready, old fellow? I'm perishing for a square meal."

"Certainly! Certainly!" Kaliko answered politely. "But first introduce me to your friends. I've been watching you through my exspectacles for an hour."

"Exspectacles!" exclaimed Betsy. "Well, I

was wondering how you knew we were here." With a proud smile Kaliko held out the pink glasses and explained how they worked and, while the little Prince and Betsy were still examining his specs, the Gnome King begged them to sit down and tell him the whole story of their adventures.

"For I'm quite sure," surmised Kaliko looking curiously from one to the other, but longest at Carter Green, "I'm quite sure you've been having some amazing adventures."

Betsy nodded vigorously and Carter grinned from ear to ear, which seemed to surprise Kaliko very much. Then, seating herself in a little rock rocking chair, Betsy told how the Hungry Tiger had been carried to Rash, of her meeting with the Vegetable Man and the strange manner in which they had arrived in the same Kingdom. Then she went on with Prince Evered's story, told how he had been deprived of his throne and robbed of the three Rash rubies.

As Betsy described the magical powers of the stolen gems, the Gnome King leaned forward with sudden interest and as the little girl explained how the Vegetable Man had come into possession of one of the lost rubies, Carter saw a surprised look flash between Kaliko and his Chief Chamberlain. Then he saw the Gnome King slip a small ring from his finger and hide it in a crevice of his throne. None of the others noticed Kaliko's action at all. Reddy was too interested in the Gnome's curious cavern to bother about any possible danger, the Hungry Tiger's eyes had closed in a momentary doze and Betsy, herself, seemed to have the greatest confidence in the King.

"I'll have to watch out for all of us," decided Carter, hurriedly wiping the mold from his nose. And while Betsy continued her story, the Vegetable Man began to examine the King's cavern with great care. "We may have to leave in a hurry," thought Carter nervously.

"Lend me those exspectacles," mumbled the Hungry Tiger sleepily, as the little girl told Kaliko their intention of returning to the Emerald City as soon as they could and having Ozma restore Reddy to his throne. "Lend me those exspectacles." When the little Prince of Rash held them up before the Hungry Tiger's eyes, he gave a roar of delight.

"What do you see?" asked Reddy curiously.

"What do I see?" purred the Hungry Tiger licking his chops. "Why, I see that lunch is ready at last. Come on fellows!"

"He's right," chuckled Kaliko, taking back his glasses. "For I ordered it an hour ago. This way my dear." Taking Betsy's arm, the Gnome King led the way to his crystal dining hall where one table was set cozily for four, and another, apparently for a dozen. "I haven't forgotten your tremendous appetite, you see,"

115

smiled Kaliko, waving toward the low table along which roasts of beef and legs of lamb were ranged in a tempting row. The Hungry Tiger gave a sigh of satisfaction, and without waiting for a knife, fork or napkin, began to munch his way hungrily down the table. For Betsy and the little Prince, Kaliko had prepared an alluring luncheon of fried chicken, sweet potatoes and peach pie. At the Vegetable Man's place stood a sparkling glass of root beer.

"I didn't suppose you'd care to eat," observed Kaliko tactfully, "but I was sure you would enjoy our National drink."

Carter was so touched by the Gnome King's thoughtfulness that he began to reproach himself for his unkind suspicions.

Kaliko, himself, ate sparingly of a hot mud pie and swallowed a cup of scalding black rock coffee and, while ten little nimble gnomes waited on the table, he and Betsy talked over old Oz times and discussed means of crossing the Deadly Desert.

"I don't know how you feel," yawned the Hungry Tiger, when he had finally worked his way to the end of his long table, "but I feel like a nap."

Betsy and the little Prince admitted that they were tired, too, and immediately Guph showed them to a splendid suite of guest caverns, just off the throne room. The Vegetable Man slammed his door hard, then opened it quite noiselessly. Just as he had expected, the two gnomes had their heads close together. Now, when it comes to hearing there is nothing so fine as a corn ear and what Carter heard through his made him tremble with indignation.

"If you weren't such a miserable mole," muttered Guph bitterly, "you'd get that other ruby!"

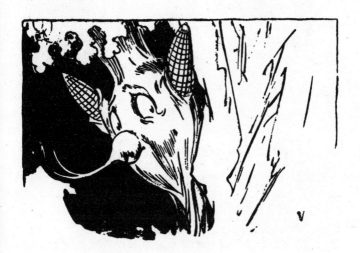

CHAPTER 11

The Second Rash Ruby

"I TOLD you there was a strange power in that ruby when you bought it from the fisherman," hissed Guph. "No ruby has an R carved in the side without some reason. It is undoubtedly one of the magic rubies of Rash—the one protecting the holder from danger by water."

Several days before Betsy's arrival, an old Ev fisherman had brought a sparkling square ruby to the Gnome King. He had found it in a fish he had drawn up in his nets and, knowing

Kaliko's fondness for jewels, had taken it straight to the King. Kaliko at once purchased the stone and had it set in a small ring—the same ring Carter had seen him slip into the rock throne. "If you had the courage of a flea," grumbled Guph, "you'd steal the ruby this vegetable person discovered and become a real power in the land."

"But it wouldn't be right," objected Kaliko, mopping his brow with his gray kerchief. "Besides, Ozma would hear of it and come with her army to conquer us."

"How could she if you had the two Rash rubies?" argued Guph. "How would she ever know? We'll just destroy all these rubbishy travellers and that will be the end of it. Where's the ring now?" he inquired anxiously.

"Safe enough," answered Kaliko, glancing over his shoulder. "I took it off as soon as Betsy mentioned the rubies. I was afraid she would notice it."

"Come on then," urged Guph coaxingly. "Can't you be a little bad for once. Tisn't natural for a gnome to be good all the time and where does all this goodness get you? Show you're a real gnome for once and forget all this mortal stuff you learned from Betsy Bobbin."

As Guph continued his wicked pleading, Carter stood frozen to the spot, his corn ears waving to and fro with wrath and indignation. He longed to snatch the precious ruby from its hiding place and dash back to warn the others.

But the gnomes were so close, he dared not move. But all at once Kaliko came to a decision and began to hurry toward a small door.

"I will consult the wizard," muttered the Gnome King in a weak whisper. "Come, let us see what the wizard thinks about this." Taking Guph's arm, Kaliko went pattering down the rocky hallway. In one leap, the Vegetable Man reached the great throne, found the ruby ring and dropped it into his leather pouch. He was about to return to his companions when the King's exspectacles, lying on the arm of the throne, attracted his attention. Clapping them hurriedly upon his nose, he rushed toward the cavern occupied by the little Prince of Rash. But halfway there he gave a great leap.

"Great cauliflowers!" gasped Carter. As plainly as you see the pictures in this book, he saw Guph thumping the little boy on the head with a pickaxe.

"Stop! Stop!" screamed the Vegetable Man, dashing into the cavern like a whirlwind. Off flew the King's exspectacles and splintered into bits on the floor, and his entrance was so noisy, Evered jumped up in a fright from the couch where he had been sleeping.

"What's the matter?" he demanded, feeling around sleepily for his sword.

"Matter!" coughed Carter, "Wasn't that rogue Guph in here?" The Prince shook his head and, looking into the next cavern, Carter saw Betsy curled up peacefully on a green sofa

and from the cave beyond came the resounding snores of the Hungry Tiger. "Nothing's happened at all," yawned Reddy.

"It was the exspectacles," puffed Carter, catching a glimpse of the pink splinters of glass at his feet.

"Do you know what is going to happen, my Rash young friend? That scalawag of a gnome intends to bang you over the ears with a pick-axe. I saw him with my own eyes and Kaliko's specs!"

"Bang me with a pick-axe!" shuddered Evered, jumping up in alarm, as Carter ran to waken Betsy and the Hungry Tiger. As fast as he could, the Vegetable Man told them all he had overheard, and showed them the ruby ring Kaliko had slyly hidden away from them. Their pleasure at recovering the second ruby was entirely spoiled by the treachery of the Gnome

King and, scarcely looking at it, Reddy thrust the ring into his pocket.

"I can run the fastest," panted the Hungry Tiger. "Jump on my back, all of you and I'll make a sprint for safety." Almost as one, the three leaped on the Hungry Tiger's back, Carter leaving his wheel-barrow with a sigh, and arming himself with the spade he had picked from the Indus Tree.

But as the Hungry Tiger dashed through the door into the throne room, Guph and his entire army came swarming through another entrance. Kaliko, himself, was nowhere in sight. He had delegated Guph to secure the Rash ruby and dispose of the travellers. Then, thought the Gnome King, if any trouble arose afterward, Guph would be held responsible.

But Guph did not intend to have any trouble afterward. He meant to destroy the travellers so utterly that not even Ozma, with her magic, would be able to discover what had become of them. Therefore, when the wicked little elf saw his four victims preparing to escape, he gave a loud screech, hurled himself at the Hungry Tiger, and brought his pick-axe down with all his might upon the head of the little Prince. It might have been a feather for all the impression it made upon Reddy. And while Betsy and Carter ducked back in dismay, the gnomes rushed at them in a body and simply rained blows upon their heads and shoulders. But the blows fell as harmlessly as an April

shower and when Carter realized this, he began
laying about with his spade so briskly that the
enemy went down in heaps.

"One of the rubies is protecting us," whispered Prince Evered, pulling out his sword.
"Take that you gray robber!" And bringing the
sword down on Guph's shoulders he stretched
him flat upon the rocks. At the same moment,

the Hungry Tiger, gathering himself for a
spring, leaped entirely over the gnome army
and, charging out the first door he came to,
raced down a long dismal tunnel. They could
hear the gnomes scampering after them and,
redoubling his speed, the Hungry Tiger fairly
flew down the dim corridor. When a sudden
turn brought him up against a swinging door,
he went through like a shot and out upon a
huge rocky cliff.

"Whoa! Whoa!" quavered Carter, jerking the Hungry Tiger frantically by the tail.

"Stop! Stop!" implored Betsy and Reddy both together. No wonder! Bubbling up from the cliff and hurling itself down over the rocks below, was a shimmering sheet of flame, the highest fire-fall, to be perfectly exact, in the whole of Kaliko's Kingdom. But the Hungry Tiger could no more stop himself than a barrel rolling down hill. With a roar that loosened three rocks and a boulder, he plunged over the cliff and down the fire-fall itself.

"Ruby! Ruby!" moaned the Vegetable Man, clutching Betsy and the little Prince. "Do your work!" The roar of the flames drowned out every other sound and green and yellow tongues of fire licked out at the travellers as they were hurled downward. But so powerful was the Rash Ruby, they were harmless as spring zephyrs, while the stones and rocks against which they bumped and bounded seemed soft as pillows. The tiger was falling head first, and somehow the three riders managed to keep on his back and hang together. Just before they reached the bottom and swirled down into the pool of flames at the base of the fire-fall, Carter lost his hold on Reddy's belt. He soon regained it, but not quickly enough.

"My ears burn," complained the Vegetable Man, as the Hungry Tiger struggled through the flaming torrent toward the shore.

"What's that?" questioned Betsy, sniffing the

air suddenly. At the same moment they were simply covered with a shower of crisp white flakes.

"My ears!" moaned the Vegetable Man, in grief-stricken tones. "They've popped!" This on top of all the other shocks was almost too much, and when the tiger had dragged himself out of the fiery stream and scrambled up the steep bank, they all dropped down upon the steaming rocks and simply panted with exhaustion.

"First time I ever came down a fire-fall," puffed Reddy, gazing fearfully at the tumbling torrent of flames.

"Well, it's the last time I ever come down one," growled the Hungry Tiger. "If it hadn't been for that ruby of yours we'd all have been nicely toasted by now. As it is—" The Hungry Tiger looked sorrowfully at the Vegetable Man.

"The best ears I ever had," groaned Carter, feeling the husks that were left to him.

"Did it hurt?" asked Betsy sympathetically. But the Vegetable Man made no reply.

"He can't hear you," explained the Hungry Tiger gloomily. "If I had that Gnome King I'd eat him."

"He *didn't* turn out very well," admitted Betsy sadly. "But never mind. Reddy has another ruby and we're in the upstairs world again."

"That's so! Maybe we're nearer the Emerald City than we think," rumbled the Hungry Tiger. "Let's look around a bit and see." Motioning for Carter to follow, and still feeling depressed over Kaliko's treachery and the Vegetable Man's sad loss, they started across the stony country edging the Gnome King's dominions.

"It's funny Ozma doesn't help us," whispered Betsy to the little Prince of Rash, as Carter storde gloomily and silently beside them. "I've been away from the Emerald City two days now and she must be wondering where I am and they have certainly missed the Hungry Tiger by this time."

"But how would Ozma know where to look for you?" asked Reddy.

"The Magic Picture would show her," answered Betsy, and quickly explained the most magic of Ozma's possessions. This curious painting hangs in the royal palace, and when Ozma wishes to know where her friends are and what they are doing she has but to stand before it and request them to appear. Immediately they flash into view, the picture showing just where they are and what they are doing at the time. More than once, Ozma had saved her subjects from serious disaster by consulting the Magic Picture, and it did seem strange that she had not looked for Betsy and the Hungry Tiger.

While Betsy and the little Prince were still puzzling over it, they stepped across the rocky borders of the Gnome King's dominion into a pleasant farming country and they were all so relieved to find themselves once again in more natural surroundings that they stopped worrying and began to enjoy themselves. The fields of potatoes and cabbages were especially cheering to Carter Green, and when they came up on a waving field of corn, he gave a joyful shout and sprang lightly over a fence.

"Wait!" he called gaily holding up both hands. "Wait till I pick a couple of ears!"

CHAPTER 12

Immense City

WHEN the Vegetable Man returned with his new corn ears, nicely adjusted, everyone felt more cheerful.

"Can you hear?" asked the Hungry Tiger curiously.

Carter nodded. "I think they're even better than the last pair," he confided happily. "It isn't everyone who can pick a new ear when his old one pops or wears out. Not so bad being a Vegetable Man, eh, Betsy, my dear?"

"No," agreed the little girl thoughtfully, "and you haven't taken root for a long time, have you Carter?"

The Vegetable Man grinned. "Haven't had a chance," he chuckled merrily. "We haven't stayed in one place long enough for that. I hope the next country we come to is calm and quiet and that I can pick up a cart and some fresh vegetables."

"I hope we can pick up a square meal," roared the Hungry Tiger, licking his whiskers hungrily.

"*I* hope there's some magic!" Clasping her hands, Betsy looked around expectantly. "Then we could cross the Deadly Desert and go home. I kinda miss Dorothy and Ozma," she acknowledged wistfully. "And I'd like to see Hank."

"Well, I hope we find the last ruby," exclaimed Prince Evered. "The one Kaliko had must have been the ruby that protected one from danger by water. You said he bought it from a fisherman, Carter?"

"Yes," mused the Vegetable Man. "It must be the one Irashi flung into the river, while the one I found was the ruby that protects from danger on the earth and under the earth. Look how it saved us from the pick-axes and the fire-fall!"

"Then the only one left to find is the ruby that protects you from danger in the air," reflected Betsy thoughtfully. "Do you spose we'll have to fly up in the air to find it?"

"Not if I have anything to say about it," growled the Hungry Tiger, shaking his handsome head. "Falling is bad enough; flying would

turn my whiskers perfectly white. We'll stay on the earth if we can, and travel back to Oz by the fastest route we can find. Then Ozma can settle affairs in Rash, discover the where-abouts of the last ruby and restore Reddy to his throne."

"Can Ozma do all that?" marveled the little Prince wonderingly.

"Ozma can do anything," Betsy answered proudly. "Just wait till you see the Emerald City and Scraps and the Scarecrow."

"Tell me about them," begged the little Prince eagerly, and as the Hungry Tiger padded comfortably down the long sunlit lanes, Betsy told Reddy all about the jolly inhabitants of Oz. The Vegetable Man listened attentively, too, his new ears a bit forward and a dreamy expression in his kindly blue eyes. But right in the middle of a description of Tik Tok, the metal man, he gave a bounce of surprise.

"Spinach!" spluttered Carter Green explosively.

"Where?" inquired the Hungry Tiger, coming to an abrupt stop and blinking around longingly. He was not very fond of spinach, but even spinach would taste better than nothing.

"I didn't mean spinach exactly," mumbled the Vegetable Man hurriedly. "But look!" Pointing his twig-like finger to a bend in the road, Carter directed their attention to a weather beaten sign.

"Beware the Ants!" advised the sign mysteriously.

"Oh, I hope they're not red ants," murmured Betsy, anxiously. "Red ants bite!"

"Who's afraid of ants?" cried Reddy disdainfully. "All you have to do is tread on 'em."

"That's right," agreed the Hungry Tiger. "I'm surprised at you, Carter, stopping us for a little thing like that."

"But suppose there were millions of them," shuddered the Vegetable Man uneasily. "I'd be a feast for ants."

Betsy looked troubled, but the Prince of Rash, slapping his pocket suddenly, reminded her of the Rash rubies.

"The rubies will protect us no matter what happens," declared Reddy, confidently.

"As soon as you see an ant, jump on my

131

back," advised the Hungry Tiger calmly. "Then we'll all stick together and I'll run like sixty."

Carter shook his head and muttered unhappily to himself. He could not help remembering the sad accident to his ears. They all kept their eyes glued to the road for the first sign of the ants, the Hungry Tiger tip-toeing along almost as if he were walking on eggs. They were all so intent upon the road beneath their feet that they never thought of the road ahead at all. Then Betsy, suddenly looking up to see whether any towns or villages were visible, gave a shrill scream and clasped her arms round the tiger's neck.

"Ants?" quavered Carter, leaping upon the Hungry Tiger and fastening both hands in Reddy's belt. Betsy was too shocked for speech, and it was the Hungry Tiger, himself, who answered Carter's query.

"Ants!" coughed the Hungry Tiger, trembling like a leaf, "Giants!" And swinging about like a pivot, the terrified beast raced off in the opposite direction. But the Giants had already seen them. There were four of the huge creatures, and Betsy, glancing fearfully over her shoulder saw the smallest—a perfectly tremendous little girl Giant—beginning to gain on them. The Hungry Tiger did his best, but who could hope to outdistance a creature whose every step covered a city block?

"Father! Father!" shrilled the little Giant, in a voice that shook the hills, "see that darling little kitten!" Before the luckless travellers had time to plan, think, or act, a great hand came snatching downward and seized the Hungry Tiger by the scruff of the neck. Up went the tiger, off went the three riders and, turning seven somersaults, landed together in a hay field. By the time they had picked themselves up, the Giants were a mile down the road.

"They're worse than gnomes," sputtered Carter indignantly. "Called the Hungry Tiger, a kitten! Did you hear that? It's a wonder that great girl didn't break us to bits."

"She would have if we had not had the rubies," panted Evered, picking up his sword. "We must have fallen a quarter of a mile. Weren't you scared Betsy?"

Betsy shivered, but recovering herself quickly

ran out into the road and tried to catch a last glimpse of the Hungry Tiger. "We'll have to go after them," she cried. "That girl needn't think she can have the Hungry Tiger for a kitten. Why, he must be furious."

"I'm glad she didn't pick me for a pet," exclaimed Carter, walking briskly up and down to keep from taking root. "Let's go on, Betsy. Maybe the Giants live around here somewhere and maybe we can help the Hungry Tiger to escape."

"I'm not afraid of Giants," asserted Reddy, in a slightly shaky voice. "Come on, we've the Rash rubies to protect us." Trying to keep up their courage and assuming a bravery they were very far from feeling, the three adventurers started off in the direction the Giants had taken.

"Well, I hope we don't meet any more," sighed Betsy, pressing closer to the Vegetable Man, "and I hope we find the Hungry Tiger before night time."

The sun had set, and in the gray twilight the trees and bushes took on fearsome shapes and forms. Keeping close together, and conversing in scared whispers, they hurried anxiously along. Soon large and disturbing signs began to appear on both sides of the road.

"This country belongs to the Big Wigs. Keep Out!" advised the signs.

"Big Wigs!" breathed Betsy nervously, "Why, they must be the giants."

"See how high the fences are, and the trees are so tall I cannot even see the tops," gasped Reddy. Feeling smaller than ever, the two children and Carter tip-toed down the long dark lanes and presently came to the Giant City, itself. All they could see was a grim gray wall, stretching up toward the sky. Hanging in niches of the wall at regular distances were great yellow lanterns and traced on the wall itself in flaming letters stood the town's name.

"Immense City," quavered the Vegetable Man, in a choked voice. "Well, I should say it was!"

"If there were only a gate," mourned Betsy, "we might peek through. Oh, dear, I do hope the Hungry Tiger is safe."

"He's safe enough," groaned Carter, looking sadly at the great wall, "but how are we ever to get in to him?" The only entrance to Immense City seemed to be a huge stone door in the center of the wall, and it was locked and bolted with bars as big as telegraph poles. Over the wall came a confused murmur of voices, the rumble of wheels and a muffled sound of music, while drifting down to the tired, hungry travellers came the delicious smell of a hundred giant dinners cooking.

"Just one giant biscuit would be enough for us," sighed Betsy, sniffing the air wistfully. "I'll bet it would be as big as you are Reddy."

"What's the use of wishing," sighed the little Prince gloomily. "We can never climb over the wall and there's nothing to eat on this side. I almost wish we had stayed Down Town!"

Both children looked so down-hearted that Carter saw at once that something must be done. So, bidding them keep close together, the Vegetable Man went off in search of supper. The lanterns from the city wall spread their radiance for miles around and it was not long before Carter came to a great apple orchard. Climbing the trees was impossible, but scattered about on the ground were apples the size of pumpkins. Taking one of the smallest, the Vegetable Man hurried back to the others. In spite of its size, the apple was of delicious flavor. Reddy cut it into slices with his sword and he and Betsy grew so merry over their strange supper that Carter felt well repaid for his trouble.

"To-morrow," promised the Vegetable Man gaily, "We will find a way into the city and rescue our old friend."

"And to-night?" queried Betsy, uneasily.

"To-night we will rest," answered Carter calmly, as if sleeping under the walls of a giant city were quite a usual affair. Gathering leaves and twigs, he made Betsy and Evered comfortable beds in the shelter of a giant elm. For himself, he collected a pile of rocks. "So I'll not take root," he explained with a wink. The leafy beds were so soft and Betsy and Reddy so weary, they soon fell asleep, but Carter on his rocky couch never closed his eyes.

CHAPTER 13
Beside the Wall

THE bright sun awakened Betsy and Reddy next morning. Betsy had been dreaming of the Emerald City and was but half awake. Rubbing her eyes, she stared in bewilderment at the high walls of Immense City.

"Oh, dear!" mused the little girl, heaving a sigh of disappointment, "We're still here, aren't we?"

"I should say we are," answered Carter, "and when you think of all we've been through it's quite a miracle, Betsy my child, to even be here." Carter had brushed back his celery tops, perked up his ears, washed his red cheeks in the brook and looked fresh as only a Vegetable Man may.

"I wonder if the Big Wigs ever use that door," yawned the little Prince of Rash, rolling over sleepily.

"Just what I was wondering," murmured Carter. "Now my plan is this. Let us watch the door carefully. Then, when it opens, we will slip in unnoticed and look around for the Hungry Tiger. But we must be mighty careful not to get run over or trodden upon by the Giants."

Betsy turned a trifle pale at mention of the Giants, but Reddy hastened to reassure her. "I'll take care of you, Betsy," promised the little Prince boldly, "and the rubies will help even if the Giants do catch us."

Somewhat comforted, but not absolutely convinced, Betsy ran over to the brook, and after she and Reddy splashed their hands and faces with the cool water and took a long drink from a nearby spring, they both felt quite adventurous and cheerful.

"We'll not bother about breakfast," decided Carter, "for I've a notion there'll be plenty inside."

"Do you really s'pose they'll open the gate?" asked Betsy, quite excited at the prospect of entering a giant city.

"Well, the four Big Wigs we met on the road must have come out that way," observed Carter, blinking up at the enormous tulip trees surrounding the Big Wig Town. Each leaf was large as a person and Carter was about to pick one up from the ground and fashion it into a hat for Betsy, when a perfect shower of rocks came flying over the wall. While none actually hit the three travellers they were so startled by the suddenness of the attack that they stood frozen to the spot. Then Carter, seizing Betsy, darted behind a tree. Before Reddy could join them, a flock of monstrous pigeons swooped down from the wall and began pecking greedily at the rocks.

"Why they're giant crumbs," cried Betsy, peering around the tree in astonishment. "Did you ever see such big birds? Why, they're big as ostriches!"

"Bigger!" gulped Carter, anxiously motioning for Reddy to hide himself. But just then one of the pigeons, taking the little boy for a crumb or a tempting little bug, snapped him up in its bill and soared over the wall of the city.

"Stop! Come back! Help! Help!" shouted Carter Green, while Betsy jumped up and down with terror and astonishment. But the pigeons on the ground continued to peck at the crumbs and the pigeon that had carried off the little Prince was as gone as yesterday.

"Will it eat him?" cried Betsy tearfully. "Oh Carter, what shall we do now?" And with Reddy and the Hungry Tiger both gone, things looked dark, indeed. The Vegetable Man had no idea what to do nor how to do it but,

determined to comfort Betsy, he began talking so confidently and cheerfully that she soon dried her tears.

"No harm can come to Reddy, for he still has the Rash rubies," he reminded her gaily. "And all we have to do is wait here till someone opens the door in the wall. Then we'll find the Hungry Tiger and Reddy and continue our journey to Oz."

After the pigeons had flown away, Carter rolled one of the giant crumbs over to the little girl. Breaking off the crust, which was a bit stale, they found the inside soft and fresh and, while it was not exactly the breakfast she would have chosen, Betsy managed to satisfy her hunger. Then, sitting down on the twisted roots of a tulip tree, they waited impatiently for the doors of Immense City to open.

But nothing of the kind happened, and as the morning wore away Carter grew terribly uneasy. He was more anxious about Reddy and the Hungry Tiger than he cared to admit. Afraid to leave the spot for fear the door would open while they were away, the two stared anxiously at the wall. But it was a weary business and more and more Betsy began to wonder why Ozma did not come to her assistance. There were plenty of crumbs for Betsy's lunch and supper, but as night drew on and still no one came to open the door, Carter decided to take matters into his own hands. Slowly a plan was forming in the Vegetable Man's mind, and as the moon rose up over the tulip trees, he explained it carefully to Betsy Bobbin.

"To-night," announced Carter in a firm voice, "I will plant my feet close to the walls of the city. In giant soil I ought to grow very rapidly and by morning should reach the top of the wall. Then I will bend over and grow downward till I touch the ground on the other side."

"But what will become of me?" cried Betsy, looking at Carter with frightened eyes.

"You will grow with me," and the Vegetable Man calmly. "I will take you in my arms and we will grow up together."

"Then what?" asked the little girl doubtfully. "How will you grow down again?"

"I won't!" answered the Vegetable Man

142

resignedly, "but I'm not important, Betsy dear, and shall doubtless make some sort of useful vine or tree."

"I don't want you to be a vine," wailed the little girl in dismay. "Please don't be a vine and leave me all alone."

"But we must think of the others," Carter pointed out gently. "Once inside the city, you will find the Hungry Tiger and Reddy and with the help of the Rash rubies manage to escape. When you reach Oz perhaps Ozma will find a way to have me transported and transplanted in the Emerald City. I'd like to be near you, Betsy," sighed the Vegetable Man wistfully.

In vain Betsy reasoned, argued and coaxed, Carter's mind was fully made up. It grew darker and darker as they talked, and just as the lanterns flashed out from the Big Wig wall the Vegetable Man picked her up in his arms and ran over to the great barred door. Standing as close to the wall as he could squeeze, Carter set Betsy on his shoulder and resolutely planted his feet in the soft earth and gazed up into the darkness.

"Now then," chuckled Carter, assuming a jaunty and care-free air to reassure the little girl, "I'm rooting for you, Betsy dear, and tomorrow we'll grow over the top."

But at that instant there was a loud thump on the other side of the wall. With a screech, the door crunched open and a giant foot was thrust through.

"Betsy! Betsy!" bellowed a terrible Big Wig voice. "Where are you, Betsy?"

Betsy Bobbin stared at the Vegetable Man, and he stared at the giant foot. There was something familiar about that foot—but what was it?

CHAPTER 14
The Airman of Oz

BETSY had been perfectly right in supposing Princess Ozma would soon discover her absence from the castle. Dorothy had gone home with the Tin Woodman, so, of course, knew nothing about it, but when Betsy did not appear for breakfast Ozma immediately sent Jellia Jam, her small maid-in-waiting, upstairs to search for her. Ozma, herself, hurried out into the garden, thinking Betsy might be gathering a breakfast bouquet. Shading her eyes, Ozma looked in every direction, but there was no sign of Betsy anywhere. She was about to return to the castle when a loud bump sounded just behind her. Spinning about, Ozma saw the strangest sort of figure, sprawled over her favorite rose bush. It was four times the size of a regular man, the body something like a tremendous sausage, with a round, balloon-shaped head and pudgy arms and legs. While Ozma was trying to determine what kind of being it was, the huge creature rose with a bounce and came clumping toward her.

"I told Zeph there were people at the bottom of the air!" puffed the stranger gleefully. "Here is one now. I'll take it straight back to the sky for proof."

Ozma had just time to notice that he wore heavy iron boots, when he bent over and, tucking her under his arm as if she had been a package of sugar plums, kicked off one boot and then the other and soared, like a balloon released from its string, straight up toward the sky. It was all so unexpected and breath-taking for several minutes Ozma was perfectly para-lyzed. Then, glancing down and seeing her lovely castle fading to a mere speck below, she began to squirm and struggle and pound with both hands upon the arm of her captor.

"Take me back! Put me down!" commanded Ozma, imperiously. "How dare you carry me off like this?" But her tiny fists made no impression on the great fellow. He seemed to be constructed of some tough silken substance, and from the way he dented in when she poked him, Ozma concluded he was filled with air. "Like a balloon," thought the Princess. "Oh, please! Please stop!" she called despairingly.

The voice of the little fairy came wafting faintly up to the airman and, with an interested sniff, he took Ozma from beneath his arm and held her on a level with his nose. The quick change made her exceedingly dizzy, and while she recovered herself he examined her most attentively. He was swimming in the air all the time, with his feet in a strange climbing motion, and their flight upward never slackened during the conversation that followed.

"What a pretty little creature it is," mused the airman half aloud. His voice was so kind and his face so round and jolly that Ozma took heart and began begging him to return her to the earth.

"I am a Princess," she explained earnestly, "and anything may happen to my Kingdom while I am away. Something *has* happened already." Breathlessly she began to tell of the disappearance of Betsy Bobbin and of the perils that might overtake her in a magic country like Oz. But the airman seemed more interested in Ozma's voice and appearance than in her story.

"Why it's talking airish," he chuckled with a pleased grin. "And what splendid proof a Princess will be when I deliver my lecture next month before the Cloud Country Gentlemen. Fellow Airmen! I shall say, It has long been a matter of dispute as to whether any life exists

in the lower levels of the air, but now the question is settled for all time. The earth is undoubtedly populated by small fragile Princesses like this." Here he paused and held Ozma up as if displaying her to an imaginary audience.

"Oh! Oh! Please stop and listen to me!" entreated Ozma. Then she gave a great gasp, for without warning the sky darkened and in their swift flight they barely escaped the gleaming point of a star.

"Don't be alarmed," murmured the airman, feeling the little fairy tremble in his grasp. "Night has fallen. The higher we go, the faster time flies. It will be daylight in a few moments. That's one of the advantages of high living," he continued comfortably. "One grows up so quickly and time flies so fast we never are bored. See, it is to-morrow already!"

148

"To-morrow!" wailed Ozma, blinking in the sudden sunlight that came flooding through the clouds. "How dreadful! Oh dear, Mr. Balloon Man, do take me back to my castle."

"Atmos is my name," announced the airman a bit stiffly, "Atmos Fere. I am a skyman, and I could not take you back even if I wanted to, for I have left my diving boots on the earth. You'll grow used to it up here," he assured her, and turning on his back began to float lazily toward a long purple cloud, still holding Ozma aloft so he could more easily observe her.

"A most interesting specimen," he muttered over and over, squinting at the little fairy approvingly.

"I'm not a specimen, I'm a Princess!" declared Ozma indignantly. "I do not wish to live in the sky. Oh, dear! Oh, my! What will become of Oz while I am away?"

"Now you're unreasonable," sighed Atmos reproachfully. "What will become of my lecture if I let you go? Do you think for one instant any air body would believe me when I told them there were living creatures at the bottom of the air? I must have proof and you are my proof, little Princess. You should feel honored to have been discovered by a well-known explorer. You shall have an air castle all to yourself and the lecture will only take a few years of your time. Hello, it's night again!"

And sure enough it was. Shivering in the darkness, Ozma began to fully realize the awful perils of her position. It might be years before she saw her old friends and the lovely Emerald City again.

Being a fairy, Ozma knew that she herself would not grow older, but what might not happen in Oz during her long absence? Clasping her hands desperately, the little Princess tried to think of some way to help herself, and as the sun came flashing through the clouds again a dreadful plan popped into her head.

Atmos was still talking. "After the lecture, there will be a dinner," droned the airman sleepily, "that will take about seven years, I should say, though I've known sky banquets to last as long as ten."

"Ten?" moaned Ozma, with a little shudder, and steeled by the thought of a ten-year banquet, she drew an emerald pin from her dress and thrust it quickly into the airman's side. Then covering her face with both hands, she began to cry softly, for this tender-hearted little fairy had never hurt anyone in her whole gentle life and could not bear to even think of what she had done. For several seconds the airman's calm conversation continued. Then all at once he gave a great gulp.

"Princess!" gasped the airman in a faint voice, "I seem to be losing my breath!"

Ozma felt a rush of cold air past her ears, and next instant they were tumbling earthward, over and over, and over, down through clouds

and mists and great blue stretches of empty air. How she managed, during that long, dizzy fall, to keep hold of the airman's limp arm, she never knew, herself. But hold on she did and after what seemed to be hours and hours, they landed together in a feathery field of wheat. The sudden plunge downward had kept all the air from escaping from the airman, but as Ozma rolled over and saw his pitiable condition, she began to weep anew. His legs and body were perfectly limp and the air was issuing from his right arm with a shrill whistling sound.

"Save me!" panted Atmos, rolling his eyes wildly from side to side. "Save me! Can't you see I'm expiring?"

"But what can I do?" sobbed Ozma, in a panic.

151

"Tie something round my neck," directed the airman desperately. "Keep the air in my head."

Snatching the ribbon from her curls, Ozma hastened to do as he suggested, shivering a little as she pulled the ribbon tight.

"I'd like to know how this happened," moaned Atmos, as the little fairy tied the ribbon in a neat bow under his poor, wrinkled chin.

"It was my fault," confessed Ozma, covering her face so she could not see him. "I stuck you with a pin. You wouldn't let me go and I couldn't leave Oz for all those years. Oh, dear! Oh, dear! I'm so sorry!" and remorseful tears began to trickle through her fingers and drop on the airman's nose.

"Punctured—by—a—Princess!" puffed Atmos, as if he could get the idea through his head at all. "Well, who would have thought it? She looked so harmless, and sweet, too. I think I should be the one to cry," he observed presently, and as the little fairy's sobs grew more and more violent, he lifted his head and regarded her with positive alarm.

"Don't cry like that," begged Atmos uncomfortably. "It didn't hurt, you know, and I have expired in the cause of high skyence. That's a great honor, besides I should not have carried you off. Don't cry," he begged, trying frantically to rise. But the more he coaxed and blamed himself, the harder Ozma wept, so that neither

of them heard the approaching steps of a stranger.

"Hello!" cried a bluff voice suddenly. "What's the matter here? Did you bust your balloon, little girl, or what?" Glancing up, Ozma saw a tall red faced fellow in a leather apron just behind her. The head of the airman did look like a great balloon, and while Ozma quickly dried her tears, Atmos simply stared at the newcomer, almost forgetting his misfortune in his curiosity.

"What is this?" he whispered huskily. "I thought earth was inhabited by Princesses like yourself. Is this a Princess, too?"

"Hah, hah, hah!" roared the stranger, slapping his greath thigh. "Do I look like a Princess?" Then, as the curiousness of a balloon's conversing struck him, his eyes grew rounder and rounder and his mouth hung open with astonishment.

"It's an airman," explained Ozma with dignity, "and I am the Princess of Oz."

"Airman!" muttered the big fellow under his breath. "Oz? Well, I've heard of Oz, but you're a long way from home, little lady, and where on earth did you pick up this fellow?"

"He's from the sky," Ozma hastened to inform him.

"And I've had a serious accident," added Atmos, to save the little fairy from telling her part in the affair.

"You look like an accident," observed the stranger, kneeling down beside the collapsed form of the airman. "Was it a puncture or an explosion?"

"A—a puncture," sighed Atmos, with a sidelong glance at Ozma, "but what manner of earth creature are you?"

"I'm an ornamental iron worker," announced the stranger proudly. "There's my shack over yonder. Rusty Ore is my name, and say!" He rose and looked triumphantly at the little fairy. "I believe I could blow this fellow up again. I've a bellows in the shop. Shall I try?"

"Oh, could you? Would you?" begged the little Princess, clasping her hands eagerly. The more Rusty looked at lovely little Ozma, the surer he became that he could. Everyone who saw Ozma had an immediate desire to serve her, and the ornamental iron worker was no exception. Rolling the airman into a neat bundle, he slung him over his shoulder. Then, taking Ozma's hand, strode briskly across the fields.

"Have you anything to eat in your house?" asked the little Princess, skipping to keep up with Rusty's long strides. "I haven't had anything to eat for two days!"

"Two days!" bellowed the iron worker indignantly, and sweeping Ozma up into his arms, he broke into a run, so that almost before they knew it, they had reached his queer little shop.

CHAPTER 15

Rusty Ore to the Rescue

WHILE Ozma, perched on Rusty's rude bench, nibbled hungrily at the big sandwich she had brought her, Atmos looked around him with interest and frank curiosity. The little shop was filled with iron deer, fire irons, iron dogs and weather cocks, too. Rusty had placed the punctured airman on top of a scrap heap, while he went to search for his bellows, that he might blow him up.

"Is this an earth castle?" asked Atmos, as

Rusty disappeared through the doorway. "Are there many creatures like this at the bottom of the air?"

"Rusty is a man. There are plenty of men, women, children, Kings, Queens and animals down here," answered Ozma, hardly knowing how to begin to tell an airman about the real and unreal countries of the earth. "Everyone here does not live in a castle," she went on seriously. "Most people live in houses or on farms."

"What's a farm?" asked Atmos, with a puzzled frown. "Do you know, little Princess, I think I had better explore this country a bit further before I'm blown up. Think what a lecture I can give on the wonders at the bottom of the sky!"

"Why don't you?" asked Ozma, swallowing the last bite of the sandwich.

"What?" inquired Rusty, returning just then with the bellows.

"I was just remarking to the Princess that I'd like to see more of your earth before I return to the sky," confided Atmos, blinking his round eyes at the iron worker. "But as soon as I'm blown up and patched I'll fly straight upward."

"How did you manage before?" questioned Rusty, sitting down on the bench beside Ozma.

"Well," said Atmos, "a friend of mine who lives on the Mountains of the Moon, made me a pair of iron boots. These enabled me to sink through the air and walk about the bottom of the sky which you call the earth. I wanted to find out if the earth was inhabited. Putting on the boots, I dove from the tip of the Moon and landed in a strange and lovely garden, where the first object that met my eyes was the lovely little lady before us. Delighted with my find, I picked this Princess from the garden, kicked off my boots and flew back to the sky, carrying her along as proof."

"Proof?" blustered Rusty, jumping up indignantly. "How dare you steal a Princess for proof, you old rascal! What shall I do to him?" he puffed, turning angrily to Ozma.

"Oh, nothing, please do nothing!" begged the little fairy in alarm. "He did not really mean any harm and I'm down on earth again. Besides—" (Ozma's voice sank to a low whisper), "besides, I punctured him with a pin."

"You did!" exclaimed Rusty admiringly. "Well, good for you!"

"Yes!" sighed Atmos sorrowfully. "It was good for her, but exceedingly bad for me. Still, I can see now that it was wrong for me to carry her away, and if you'll find some way to blow me up and keep me down, I'll take her safely back to her castle."

"Now you're talking like a real man instead of a wind bag," said Rusty approvingly. "I'll tell you what I'll do. I'll make you a pair of iron shoes myself, blow you up, patch you up and start you in the right direction. How would that be?"

Ozma was so delighted with the iron worker's plan that she gave him a hearty hug, and as Rusty started to work on the boots at once, it was not long before they were finished and standing in the doorway to cool.

Blowing Atmos up was a ticklish and dangerous operation. Carrying the airman outside, Rusty placed him on the ground. Then, placing the bellows in his side, he began to work it slowly and carefully, while Ozma watched to see that each arm and leg had the same amount of air. Before they started, Rusty had weighted Atmos down with an iron bucket and an iron stag, but as the body of the airman filled out, he grew so light and buoyant they had to add the anchor and a couple of chains.

"Not too much, now," warned Ozma, anxiously untying the ribbon from the airman's throat. "Not too much, or he'll burst!"

But Atmos did not burst, and when Rusty saw he had exactly filled out his strange silken skin, he pulled out the bellows, clapped a neat patch over the puncture and stood back to admire this curious citizen of the air. Atmos, himself, began to bounce, swing his arms and sing aloud for pure joy.

"Excuse my singing," chuckled the airman, "but I'm full of fresh air and you have no idea how fine it feels."

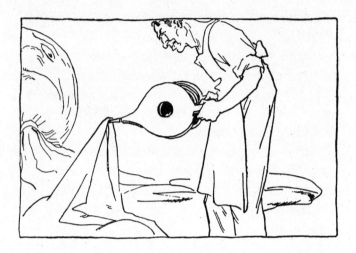

"Well, don't put on airs with us," muttered Rusty, who was really alarmed at the airman's size. "Do you think he's safe?" he whispered nervously to Ozma. Ozma nodded enthusiastically and, somewhat reassured, Rusty went off to pack her a lunch for the journey back home.

By this time, the boots had cooled and, with great difficulty, Rusty fitted them to the airman's puffy feet, released him from the iron weights and chains and helped him to rise.

Ozma watched with great interest, for she was not at all sure the boots would keep Atmos on the earth. But after a few skips and flutters the airman began to walk soberly up and down, and with a pleased smile declared himself ready to start.

Rusty was sorry to have the little Princess go, but when she explained the strange disappearance of Betsy Bobbin and how she must return at once to the Emerald City and try to discover her whereabouts in the Magic Picture, he reluctantly bade her good-bye.

"You are on the edge of the Gnome King's dominions," said Rusty, "and if you travel straight ahead you will come to the Deadly Desert. With iron boots Atmos should have no trouble crossing the burning sands, and if he carries you on his shoulder no harm will come to you."

"I have never seen a desert," said Atmos eagerly, "for there are no deserts in the sky. Come, little Princess, let us go at once." Giving Rusty a farewell embrace and thanking him again for all his kindness, Ozma ran after the airman, who had already started toward the South.

"Good-bye!" called Rusty, as they turned to wave to him from a little hill. "Be careful not to tread on her toes!"

The country through which they were passing was barren and wild and not at all interesting to Ozma, but the airman stopped and exclaimed over every tree and boulder, collecting so many leaves, flowers, sticks and small stones, that his air pockets were soon bulging.

"I'm really quite glad I was punctured," he remarked happily. "Otherwise I should have missed all this."

Ozma nodded, a bit impatiently, for she was thinking of all *she* had missed during her strange two days in the air, and wondering what had become of Betsy Bobbin.

"Maybe she's been home all the time," sighed the little Princess, "and won't she be astonished when I tell her where I have been. Oh, dear, I do wish he would hurry. If you put any more stones in your pocket you'll never be able to fly," she cautioned gently, "and if we don't walk a little faster, we'll never reach the Emerald City at all."

"That's so," puffed the airman, and straightening up he reluctantly dropped a handful of pebbles. "But walking is so monotonous. In the air, we can drift, float, swim or fly and so we never grow tired."

"It must be very nice," agreed Ozma politely, "but don't you think you could walk a little faster? We're going to have a storm," she added, glancing up at the sky, which was full of dark clouds. "Oh, Atmos, let's run and maybe we'll reach a house before it breaks."

"Breaks?" panted the airman, clumping clumsily after the light-footed little fairy. "What will it break? Us?"

"Don't you ever have any storms in the sky?" called Ozma over her shoulder.

Atmos shook his head solemnly. "We're above all that sort of thing," grunted the airman, trying his best to keep up with Ozma. "Dear me, how dreadfully disagreeable." The sky had grown dark by this time and the rain was falling in torrents. Blinding flashes of lightning and

loud crashes of thunder added to the confusion
and when large hail stones came pelting down
upon their heads, Atmos stopped in positive
alarm.

"Princess! Princess!" choked the airman,
groping toward Ozma in the dark, "Get me out
of this or I'll be punctured!"

"If I only had my magic belt!" gasped Ozma,
pushing back her wet hair, "I could wish us
both to the Emerald City. Oh, dear, I do wish
there was a house somewhere!"

Scarcely had the words been spoken before a
house sprang up at the little girl's feet—so
suddenly, in fact, that it tumbled her over
backwards. The morning before she left her
castle, Ozma had slipped one of the Wizard's
wishing powders into her pocket.

But, shoe strings and button hooks! The
little girl had not been careful to say what kind
of house she wanted and there, perched askew
on the dripping rocks, stood a dog house. While
Atmos stared at it in a daze, thinking it, too,
had fallen from the sky, and Ozma picked
herself up in astonishment, a cross doggie face
appeared in the doorway.

"Gr—woof!" rumbled the dog threateningly.
Where he had been wished from I cannot say,
but the journey had been unexpected and
rough, and seeing two total strangers standing
outside, the dog immediately decided they were
responsible for the accident. Paying no attention
to the rain or hail, he dashed furiously out and

163

tried to bury his teeth in the airman's leg. Thanks to his iron boots, Atmos was not punctured, and as the dog made a spring at Ozma, the airman snatched the little fairy up in his arms and began running in a way he had not believed possible. So swiftly did Atmos run that the barks of the dog soon died away in the distance and the storm was left far behind them.

"Stop! Stop!" begged Ozma, when she could finally make the airman hear her. "Stop, Atmos dear. Atmos Fere, you're running the wrong way. Oh! Oh! Do take care, there's something queer about this country."

With a final puff, Atmos brought himself to a stop, or at least he tried to. But the earth beneath his feet was behaving most unaccountably, moving along in big brown waves and carrying him tumbling along with it. They had unluckily run into the great rolling country of the east, mentioned by a few explorers, but seldom crossed by ordinary travellers. Standing first on one foot and then the other, Atmos tried wildly to keep his balance, but in a moment a heavy mud wave struck him behind the knees and rolled him over, so that he and the little Princess of Oz were soon being buffeted along like tiny ships on an unruly ocean. When the waves broke, which they frequently did, sticks, stones, pebbles and dust showered over their heads. In fact, a more miserable mode of travel cannot be imagined.

"Let us fly," choked the frightened airman, clutching Ozma's hand. "Say the word little Princess, and I'll kick off my boots and carry you up to safety."

"No! No! Not that!" coughed Ozma in a panic. "Wait Atmos, something will turn up!"

CHAPTER 16

Reddy and the Giants

WHILE Carter and Betsy waited so impatiently outside the walls, the little Prince of Rash was having an amazing day with the Giants. After a dizzy flight through the air, the great pigeon, attracted by a bit of stale cake on the ledge of a high window, had dropped him carelessly on the sill. Fortunately for Reddy, the window was open and, squirming through, he lay panting and pale, waiting for the bird to snap him up again. But the space was too narrow, and after a few angry pecks at the pane, the pigeon flew away.

With a gulp of relief, the Prince rolled over and sat up. A delicious smell of coffee, bacon and rolls came floating upward and, glancing over the edge of the sill, Reddy saw that he was in an enormous dining hall. Far below the window stood the giant sideboard, covered with serving dishes the size of bath tubs, and seated at a huge table in the center of the room, two Giants were eating porridge with spoons as large as snow shovels. They had golden crowns upon their heads, and from the richness of their robes and the elegance of the whole apartment, Reddy guessed, and quite rightly, that he was in the castle of Immense City itself.

Waiting upon their Majesties, were four monstrous footmen, and all of the Giants wore huge white wigs, the curls of which bounced and bobbed when they walked in a truly comical fashion. Crouching in a corner of the sill, and trusting that none of the Giants would notice him, the hungry little boy watched the King and Queen toss off huge basins of coffee, devour biscuits as big as boulders and pan cakes broad enough to cover an ordinary sized table. In these immense surroundings, Reddy felt so little, lost and lonely that all thought of finding and rescuing the Hungry Tiger seemed hopeless. How was he even to reach the floor, without breaking himself to bits? Therefore he listened listlessly to the booming voices of the Big Wigs, and fervently wished himself back with the Vegetable Man and Betsy Bobbin. But a cross remark of the Giant King suddenly caught his attention and made him prick up his ears.

"That kitten," growled the Big Wig in a fierce voice, frowning across the table at the Queen, "that kitten must go! It kept me awake the entire night with its miserable meowing."

"But what will Elma do," murmured the Queen gently. "Our daughter dotes on the little creature."

"Let her find something else to dote on," puffed his Majesty indignantly. "My castle is no place for stray cats. If it's here to-morrow," continued the Giant, blowing his cheeks in and out threateningly, "I'll throw it in the pond!" Snatching up his paper, the King strode from the room, every curl in his wig expressing wrath and determination.

"Stray kitten!" gasped Reddy in relief, remembering the little Giant girl's words. "Why, that must be the Hungry Tiger!" The knowledge that his old friend was still safe and close at hand was so encouraging, the little Prince cheered up at once, for after all Reddy was a Prince and naturally brave and resourceful. If the Hungry Tiger were still in the castle, he should certainly be able to find him, and together they would devise some way of escape. The Queen, still arguing about her daughter's kitten, had waddled after her husband, and while the Big Wig footmen cleared away the breakfast dishes, Reddy tried to think of some plan to reach the floor in safety. He put his hands in his pockets, stared nervously over the edge of the sill, then gave an exclamation of glee. For his fingers had closed over the Rash rubies. The rubies! Why had he not thought of them before? If one of them had carried him safely down the furious fire-fall, why would it not help him now?

Without disturbing the dishes on the side table, the footmen had gone to the kitchen. So, closing both eyes and gritting his teeth, Reddy jumped boldly off the window ledge. He landed with a crash, splash and splutter and, opening his eyes, found himself looking through the glass sides of the Giant's water pitcher. The water was over his head, but he felt no discomfort, except a slight chill from the ice, for in his pocket was the ruby protecting him from all danger by water.

Disturbed because he had not looked more carefully before he jumped, but elated over the way the rubies were working, the little Prince rose to the top of the pitcher. Luckily for him the water reached almost to the brim, and seizing the pitcher's edge he pulled himself up and dropped easily over the side. This time he landed beside a flat plate of sizzling hot cakes and bacon, and we cannot blame him for stopping long enough to hack off a few slices of each with his sword. This, with several crumbs from the giant biscuits, made an excellent breakfast, and stuffing a large piece of pan cake in his pocket for lunch, the little boy jumped gaily off the sideboard. Thanks to the other ruby, he floated lightly as a feather down to the floor and then began his long walk to the kitchen.

His clothes were still wet and dripping from the unexpected bath, but his spirits were high and he was beginning to enjoy his strange experiences and to look forward with lively anticipation to his meeting with the Hungry Tiger. A brisk fifteen-minute walk brought him to the kitchen door and, slipping through, he saw the Big Wig servants seated at a large table. Their loud voices made his head thump, and to bring their faces into view he had to lean so far over backwards, he soon had a severe pain in his neck. But he was sure he would learn from them the whereabouts of little Elma and once he knew that, finding the Hungry Tiger would be almost easy. Compared with the Giants, Reddy was about the size of a small doll and none of the chattering Big Wigs noticed the little boy crouched behind the coal bucket. After listening to a great deal of conversation that did not interest him at all, Reddy was finally rewarded with the information he was seeking.

"Where's little Elma's tray?" wheezed a Big

Wig maid, suddenly pushing back her chair. "That girl grows lazier every day!"

"There!" grunted the cook, pointing a pudgy finger toward the dresser. "And it's high time you took it up to her, you ill-natured clod."

After exchanging a few more rude remarks, the maid picked up the tray and started toward a back stairway. Frantically, Reddy began to run after her, risking discovery by the others in his anxiety to keep her in view. But it was a hopeless race, and he had just given up in despair when the giantess came hurrying back for the salt, which she had forgotten. Almost treading on the breathless little boy, she snatched a salt shaker form the dresser and started off again, but this time, Reddy went with her.

The strings of the maid's apron reached

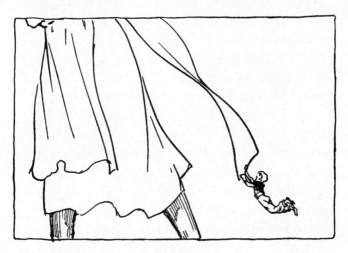

almost to the floor, and with a mighty spring the little Prince seized one of the fluttering ends and hung on for dear life. Unconscious of her passenger, the Giantess briskly mounted the stair, Reddy swinging round and round at each step and hoping heartily that the apron string would not come untied. After a very bumpy journey, the little boy found himself at the top of the stair and next instant in the presence of the little Giant Princess herself.

She was seated in a chair in the largest play room you could ever imagine, and looked extremely comical in her great white wig. Letting go the maid's apron string, Reddy dropped to the floor and creeping behind a toy block, peered around in amazement. Dolls as big as himself were strewn about the floor. Noah's Arks, toy barns, doll houses and castles as large as our own dwellings were ranged along one side of the wall and here and there were stuffed and wooden animals of just the right size for Reddy to ride. There was a toy train he longed to start and a wooden circus that made his heart thump with excitement.

"I wish Betsy were here," thought the little Prince. "Couldn't we have fun? I wish she could see these dolls!" Scarcely hearing the clatter of dishes on the tray, as the Princess greedily ate her breakfast, Reddy's eyes roved enviously over the vast collection of toys. A sudden thump, as the little Giantess jumped out of her chair, recalled him to the serious purpose of his visit. Princess Elma, with a saucer of cream in her hands, was pattering toward him calling at the top of her voice:

"Here Kitty! Kitty! Kitty! Where are you Kitty dear?"

The thought of the Hungry Tiger as a little girl's kitten was so ridiculous that Reddy chuckled in spite of himself, and when little Elma, after several unsuccessful attempts, dragged the tiger from beneath a low sofa and began dipping his nose in the cream, Reddy laughed outright.

The Hungry Tiger was growling and snarling so ferociously and Elma filling the air with such boisterous terms of endearment that neither of them heard. After a futile struggle with the Giantess, the tiger settled himself on the floor and began to lap up the cream, with an expression of unhappy and hopeless resignation. Squatting on the floor beside him, the Princess continued to shower him with vigorous caresses.

"Finish your breakfast, sweet," she cooed in a voice like a ferry-boat whistle, "then mother'll take you for a nice little ride in the doll coach!"

Reddy hoped to have a few words with the Hungry Tiger, and began to creep cautiously toward the strange pair. But just as he came within hailing distance the Hungry Tiger finished the cream, and Elma lifted him joyfully into the air. Torn between mirth and sympathy, Reddy watched the Giantess dress the indignant and struggling tiger in a doll coat and cap, tuck him unceremoniously into a doll coach and wheel him out of the nursery.

"I'll have to wait till they come back," sighed Reddy, as the doll coach went bumping down the entry and the shrill protests of the Hungry Tiger grew fainter and fainter. "And while I wait I might as well look around."

This proved so interesting that he was surprised to hear the great clock on the mantle strike twelve. As there was still no sign of the Hungry Tiger, he sensibly decided to eat his lunch. Choosing the coziest of the doll houses, he walked boldly up the front steps and into the dining room. The chairs and table were exactly the right size, and with a little chuckle of enjoyment Reddy set the table, drew up a chair and ate his piece of pan-cake in peace and comfort.

The doll house was complete in every detail, and in the kitchen cupboard the little boy found canisters of tea, coffee and sugar. There was a small gas stove that really worked, so Reddy made himself a cup of coffee and finished his lunch with a box of stale cakes he found on the dresser. Then, feeling a little sleepy, he curled up on the doll lounge in the living room and had a fine nap. After this he amused himself trying on the doll hats and coats he found in the entry closet and sliding down the curved banister.

By this time it was four o'clock, and growing

a little anxious about the Hungry Tiger, Reddy ran out of the doll house to see if the Princess had returned. But the nursery was still deserted and after trying in vain to wind up the toy engine, and taking a perilous ride on a mechanical donkey, which he did manage to start, the little boy decided to look for his friend in some of the other rooms of the palace. The toy donkey had carried him to a door leading from the play room into Princess Elma's bedroom, and slipping through, Reddy tip-toed around, examining the tall furniture and fittings with deep interest. In the center of the room, he stopped short and gave a sharp cry of astonishment. What do you think? There, looking like a toy, in these huge surroundings, stood a bed no larger than Reddy's own.

"Now what," gasped the little Prince of Rash in extreme perplexity, "is that great girl doing with a little bed like this?" There seemed no answer to the question, but a sudden clump, clump in the hall made him dash for cover. Princess Elma was coming back, and just as Reddy dove headlong into one of her slippers, she ran in, the Hungry Tiger in her arms.

"Now stay here pet!" bellowed Elma tenderly, and dropping the tiger on the floor she skipped noisily out of the room.

For a moment the Hungry Tiger lay motionless where he had fallen. The doll cap was down over his eyes, the doll coat in ribbons and Reddy could see that he had had a hard day.

When he did attempt to rise and try to run, the doll coat threw him down at every step, and the little Prince, with a cry of sympathy and relief, ran out to help him.

"Reddy!" roared the Hungry Tiger hoarsely, "How did you get here. Run boy, run, before that dreadful girl gets you, too. Look! Look at me!" he groaned forlornly. "How shall I ever hold up my head again? Run away, Reddy, I beg of you! Run, before it is too late!"

"Sh—h!" whispered Reddy warningly. "We'll run together." Cutting the cap strings with his sword and tearing off the offensive doll coat, the little boy threw both arms round the tired old tiger and gave him a tremendous hug.

"To think that I, the Hungry Tiger of Oz, should have come to this!" moaned the tiger,

two tears running down his nose. "Oh, Oh, Oh! I shall never be the same."

"Sh—h!" begged Reddy again. "To-night when the Giants are asleep, we'll escape. I still have the Rash rubies, remember." Holding them up, Reddy looked eagerly at the ruffled and doleful tiger. The sight of the rubies seemed to restore him a little.

"We can try it anyway," he mused wearily. "But, take care, here comes that awful girl back again. Hide yourself, quick!"

Reddy had just time to scramble beneath a chintz chair, when Princess Elma came bounding back, a plate of chicken in one hand and a doll bed in the other.

CHAPTER 17

The Big Wig's Secret

THE Giantess seemed astonished to find the Hungry Tiger without his wraps, and picking him up began to scold gently. She was thrusting his front paws into a doll's night dress, when a loud voice from the next room made her pause.

"Bother!" exclaimed Princess Elma, putting the Hungry Tiger down beside the plate of chicken, "I've got to take my bath. But I'll be right back."

"Don't hurry," growled the Hungry Tiger,

gnashing his teeth ferociously as Elma ran toward the Big Wig nurse, standing in the doorway.

"Why don't you bite her," asked Reddy, venturing out from beneath the chair.

"My conscience tells me it would be wrong," groaned the poor tiger. "After all, she is only a child and really means no harm."

Princess Elma was gone so long that Reddy and the Hungry Tiger had time to dine most comfortably on the plate of chicken and tell their strange experiences in the Giant Castle. The Hungry Tiger was amazed to learn how Reddy had been carried over the wall and listened eagerly to his plans for escape.

"We'll wait till mid-night," whispered the little Prince. "Then, with the Rash rubies to protect us, we'll fall all the way down the stairs and try to find our way out of the castle."

"I hope nothing has happened to Carter and Betsy," sighed the tiger mournfully. "Help me out of these horrible sleeves, boy!" But Reddy advised him to keep on the doll's gown so that Elma would suspect nothing, and reluctantly the tiger agreed. "I had no idea kittens lead such hard lives," he groaned dismally. "My ribs ache from hugging and I've been dragged around all day like a duster. Hide, Reddy, hide! Here she comes again."

Reddy lost no time in concealing himself beneath the chair, and from his hiding place he watched the Giantess kiss the Hungry Tiger good-night, and tuck him vigorously into the doll bed. Then, with a huge yawn, she walked over to her own bed—the tiny bed that had so astonished Reddy in the first place.

"How does the great creature expect to sleep in that?" thought the little boy scornfully. How, indeed? Raising her hand to her head, Elma calmly took off her huge wig, and as she did she shrank so swiftly downward that Reddy clutched the leg of the chair and clapped his hand over his mouth to keep from screaming aloud.

The Hungry Tiger, who had slept in the nursery the night before, was equally astonished at this sudden change in the Princess. Rearing up on all fours, he glared in disbelief at the little girl, who now no larger than Reddy, jumped unconcernedly into bed and pulled the covers up to her chin. The big wig, itself, grown small enough to fit a mortal-sized person, lay on the floor beside her. So surprised that he forgot all necessity for caution, Reddy rushed out from beneath the chair, but the Hungry Tiger hastily waved him back and, curling down as if nothing unusual had happened, pretended to be asleep. Fortunately the little girl had not seen Reddy, and crawling cautiously back, he sank down beneath the chair and tried to work out the puzzle.

"These Giants are frauds," decided the little boy exultantly. "Why, they're Giants only when they wear their wigs."

He longed to talk it over with the Hungry Tiger, but realizing the wisdom of hiding till all the Giants were abed, set himself patiently to wait.

It grew quieter and quieter in the Giant's Castle, and as the nursery clock tolled out twelve, the Hungry Tiger slipped noiselessly from his bed and padded softly over to the little Prince.

"She's asleep," breathed the Hungry Tiger, "and so are the rest of these bogus Big Wigs. Let's make a dash for it, my boy."

"I've been thinking," mused Reddy, as he helped the Hungry Tiger off with the giant doll dress, "I've been thinking that it will take a long time to get out of the castle and across the city. It might take us till morning."

181

"All the more reason to start at once," urged the Hungry Tiger. "Come along, let's start now."

But Reddy stood staring thoughtfully at the white wig beside Princess Elma's bed. "I've been thinking," repeated the little boy, "that if I put on that wig, I might grow into a Giant myself, run a hundred times faster than I can now and fight anyone who tries to stop us."

"Better not," shudddered the Hungry Tiger nervously. "It might stick to you. Come along, hop on my back and we'll manage somehow."

But Reddy, remembering the steepness of the Giant stair and the hugeness of the Giant city, began to creep determinedly toward Elma's bed. As he did, Elma stirred uneasily in her sleep, and alarmed, lest she wake and seize the wig before he could, Reddy snatched it from the floor and clapped it on his head. Stars! Up like a bean stalk shot the little boy, till he feared his head would crack against the ceiling. As he grew, the chairs, tables and furniture that had seemed so immense assumed an astonishing smallness. The Hungry Tiger running in a frantic circle round his feet, looked as he must have looked to Princess Elma—a very tiny and cunning kitten. Taking a long breath, Reddy leaned down, picked the tiger up and ran out of the room. The Hungry Tiger was scolding bitterly under his breath, but Reddy had to hold him up to his ear to discover what he was saying.

"Mind what you're doing," rumbled the Hungry Tiger, crossly. "I'm tired of being picked up like a bundle of rags and tossed about. Don't squeeze me either or I'll bite off your thumb. Grr—uff! I'm real mad at you!"

Chuckling a little to himself, Reddy promised to be careful, and tucking the Hungry Tiger gently beneath his arm ran down the richly carpeted hallway. He could not resist peeping into some of the rooms, and everywhere the same sight met his eyes. Tiny beds stood in the midst of gigantic bed chambers and the Giants themselves, no bigger than ordinary folk, sleeping comfortably without their wigs.

"It would be a great chance to capture the city," mused Reddy to himself and for a time wondered whether it might not be fun to try. But he was so anxious to see Betsy and Carter and continue his search for the lost ruby, that he decided to let the foolish Big Wigs rest in peace. Quickening his steps, he hurried downstairs, unbolted the doors and let himself out of the castle. Several Big Wig Guards looked at him curiously, as he hurried down the street, but they made no attempt to stop him.

"It's funny," said Reddy to the Hungry Tiger, as he panted along. "This city doesn't look large at all and it's not nearly so big nor fine as Rash."

"That's because you're a Giant now," roared the tiger, who was gradually recovering his good humor. "It looks pretty big to me. Where are we anyway?"

"Right at the gates," answered Reddy triumphantly. "Here, you, get out of the way!" The Big Wig Guard, who was asleep with his back against the wall, blinked with surprise and resentment as Reddy spun him out of his path and slid back the bolts. Then, opening the gates, Reddy darted through, calling Betsy Bobbin at the top of his voice.

"Hush!" roared the Hungry Tiger. "Be still, can't you. Do you want to scare her to death?"

We know already how frightened Betsy and the Vegetable Man really were. Failing to recognize Reddy in the huge big wig, as he came bounding through the door way, they took hands and ran for their lives.

"Come back! Come back!" pleaded the Prince of Rash, making frantic little snatches at the fleeing pair. "Stop, Carter! Stop, Betsy! Don't you know me?"

"The wig, idiot. Take off the wig," grumbled the Hungry Tiger, who was tired of being jostled up and down. "Take off the wig."

So Reddy, who had been about to lift Betsy up and explain who he was, snatched off his wig instead. In a twinkling he had shrunk down to boy-size and, releasing his hold on the Hungry Tiger, chased merrily after Carter and Betsy.

"Betsy! Betsy!" gasped the little Prince breathlessly. "Don't run away from me." When Betsy, scarcely believing her ears, looked over her shoulder and saw Reddy and the Hungry Tiger instead of a Big Wig, she spun about in perfect astonishment.

"But the Giant!" exclaimed Betsy, while Carter Green hurried forward to embrace Reddy and hug the Hungry Tiger. "What became of the Giant?"

"Here it is," coughed the Hungry Tiger, dropping Princess Elma's wig, which he had picked up when Reddy dropped it, and brought along in his teeth.

While Carter and Betsy continued to stare at them in wonder, Reddy related the history of his experience in Immense City, and told how he had stolen the wig. Then, to demonstrate its strange power, he tried it on and turned before their eyes into a Big Wig himself.

"Well," sighed Betsy Bobbin, as he took it

185

off and shrank down beside her, "I don't believe anybody in Oz is having as queer adventures as this. Do you, Carter?" The Vegetable Man shook his head positively.

"But they're turning out all right," he added cheerfully. "Here we are, all together again, with two of the lost rubies and a magic wig besides. I think we should be very happy," finished Carter, smiling at the Hungry Tiger.

"That's because you were never a kitten," roared the tiger, beginning to lick his satiny coat into smoothness again. "What I've endured at the hands of that great girl no one will ever know! Ugh! Brrr-rr!"

"Won't she have to stay little without her wig?" asked Betsy, curiously.

"Hope she does. Hope she feels just as small as I did," grumbled the Hungry Tiger vindictively. "She's far safer as she is now."

"Maybe they'll make her a new one," suggested Reddy. "Why, Betsy, they're not Giants at all—just big frauds and I'm going to keep this wig always, just to remember them by."

"Don't wear it when I'm around," groaned the Hungry Tiger, rolling his yellow eyes fiercely. "I don't want to remember 'em, and every time I look at it I'll think of the awful day I spent as a kitten."

Though it was way past mid-night, the four adventurers had so much to tell and so many plans to make for the morrow, it was a long

time before they finally settled themselves for sleep. But after Betsy had heard all over again about Princess Elma's marvelous toys and how Reddy had fallen into the giant water pitcher, the little boy and girl stretched out on the soft grass beside the road and pillowing their heads comfortably on the tender-hearted old tiger, slept soundly as tops. But Carter did not need to sleep, so perching upon a fence, he watched the moon sailing across the starry sky and kept a sharp lookout for Giants.

CHAPTER 18

The Third Rash Ruby

"IT WAS wicked of Irashi to steal the throne, but I'm almost glad he did," remarked the little Prince of Rash, as he and Betsy walked cheerfully down the road next morning. "Why, if he hadn't, I'd never have known you or Carter and the Hungry Tiger," continued Reddy, slashing at a tall weed with his sword, "and I'd never have seen all these cities and celebrities."

Much refreshed by their night's rest, the four travellers had breakfasted royally on a giant peach and set out once more for the Emerald City of Oz.

"Don't you ever feel homesick?" asked Betsy, a little wistfully. She, herself, was beginning to long for the Emerald City and a glimpse of Ozma and Dorothy and her many friends in Oz.

"Well, I would like to see old Fizzenpop," admitted Reddy with a sigh. "He must be wondering where I am, and it will be fun to be a Prince again. Still, I am glad we had all of these adventures together, aren't you Carter?"

The Vegetable Man nodded, but the Hungry Tiger did not seem at all enthusiastic. His experiences as a kitten still made him angry.

"What makes you think our adventures are over?" he rumbled irritably. "We don't even know where we are. I trust we are going in the right direction," he grunted, looking over his shoulder at Betsy. "And even if we are, how shall we cross the Deadly Desert? We have to cross the desert before we come to Oz, you know."

"Let's wait till we come to it," advised Betsy, sensibly. "And if Reddy puts on his giant wig," she added suddenly, "he can see whether we are going in the right direction and—"

"Whether there's anything to eat," put in the Hungry Tiger, who had not cared much for his breakfast. "Maybe there's a roast beef bush around somewhere," he finished hope-fully.

189

Reddy really enjoyed nothing better than shooting up into a giant. As he explained to Betsy, it made a chap see things in a much bigger way. So, quite willingly, he clapped on Elma's wig and, turning slowly, looked in all directions.

As he was now taller than the tallest tree anywhere about, he could see for miles around and it at once became apparent to those on the ground that he had made an astonishing discovery.

"What is it?" roared the Hungry Tiger, rubbing impatiently against his shins. "Something to eat? Take off that wig, you rascal! Come down here and tell us what you see."

But Reddy lifted Betsy into the air and, placing her on his shoulder, pointed excitedly toward the South. From that great height Betsy

190

could not see very distinctly, but even so the little girl gave a cry of surprise and delight. Striding down a road that would soon cross their own came a most curious figure—none other than Atmos, the airman, and pattering along hopefully at his side, the little Princess of all OZ.

"It's Ozma!" cried Betsy, nearly losing her balance. "Oh, Reddy, she's coming to help us. But who is that funny balloon man? Hurry up Reddy! Let's go meet them!"

"Like this?" boomed the Prince of Rash doubtfully.

"No," decided Betsy shaking her head. "It might scare her if you were a Giant. Put me down and take off your wig."

Almost dropping Betsy, in his excitement, Reddy pulled off his wig, and after quickly

explaining their startling discovery to the Hungry Tiger, the two children started on a run for the cross-roads.

"I hope she never finds out why I went to Rash," muttered the Hungry Tiger under his breath, as he padded hurriedly after them.

Carter followed more slowly, brushing back his celery tops and perking up his corn ears. The Vegetable Man wished to make as favorable an impression on the little Princess as possible. To Ozma, herself, and to Atmos, plodding wearily along the rough road, nothing could have been more astonishing than the sudden appearance of Betsy Bobbin and her friends.

"Why Betsy!" exclaimed the little fairy, running forward joyfully, "Where *have* you been?"

"Did you look in the Magic Picture and find us?" asked Betsy, giving Ozma an excited little hug. "Oh, Ozma, we've had such a lot of adventures and now we can all go home!"

Ozma looked doubtful, and even more surprised, for as we know perfectly well, she had not looked in the Magic Picture at all and was as lost as Betsy Bobbin.

"And I thought the earth was inhabited by Princesses," gasped the airman, looking in bewilderment from one to the other. "What odd and interesting specimens. Are you real?" he inquired, earnestly tapping Carter on the chest.

"As real as rhubarb," answered the Vegetable

Man, with a grin. "Are you? But let me introduce the famous Hungry Tiger of Oz."

"He has a beautiful mouth—" shuddered Atmos, glancing down sideways at the tiger— "Er—when it is shut? Does he bite, Mr. Er-Rhubarb?"

"Only when I'm hungry," sighed the tiger, rolling his yellow eyes mournfully up at Atmos, "And I'm hungry all the time."

"How extremely dangerous," murmured Atmos, stepping quickly behind the Vegetable Man. "Is this little boy creature with you, too?"

"Of course!" laughed Betsy, smiling up at Atmos. "He's a Prince and we're both helping him find the lost rubies so he can be the Rightful Ruler of Rash."

Betsy had been trying to explain all the happenings of the last three days and now, as prettily as she could, she introduced Carter and Reddy to Ozma, and Carter, Reddy and the Hungry Tiger to the comical airman. Then, because there was so much to explain and consider, they all sat down under a huge handkerchief tree and talked to their hearts' content.

As Betsy insisted on hearing Ozma's story first, the little Princess began it, the airman looking terribly embarrassed as she told how he had fallen from the clouds and then flown off with her. Reddy nodded sympathetically, as Ozma described her flight through the air. Having been carried off by a pigeon himself, he knew just how she felt, and when Ozma told how the days and nights flew past in the sky and how she had punctured the airman and come tumbling to earth, Carter Green was simply rooted to the spot. For the Vegetable Man, in his excitement, had forgotten to keep moving.

"But we are good friends now," put in Atmos hastily, as Reddy tugged the Vegetable Man loose. "Aren't we, little Princess?" Ozma nodded and smiled and went hurriedly on with her story. After being tossed about by the rolling country, it had at last flung them into a small lake, which was on the whole, rather fortunate, as they were nearly choked with dust. Atmos, in spite of his iron boots, floated nicely, and after they had washed off the mud, he towed the little fairy safely to shore. The sun had soon dried them off and they had taken the first road that stretched ahead.

"And you see," finished Ozma, smiling gaily at Betsy, "it was a lucky road, for it brought us straight to you."

Betsy's story, as you can well imagine took much longer, for the time had not flown as fast for the earth travellers as it had for the sky travellers. And as the little girl, helped out by Carter and Reddy and the Hungry Tiger, recounted her strange trip with Carter to Rash, the discovery of the Hungry Tiger, the wickedness of Irashi, the story of the lost rubies and the little Prince, their escape and fall Down Town—Ozma and Atmos listened with simply breathless attention. And as Betsy described their experiences with Kaliko and the tumble down the fire-fall, the airman snatched two handkerchiefs from the tree and began to mop his head with first one and then the other.

"Too strange to believe," sighed the airman weakly. "They'll never believe this in the Cloud Country."

Ozma smiled to herself at this, and decided that the airman's lecture would last several centuries if he tried to include Betsy's story with his own. Betsy was so out of breath by this time, Reddy took up the tale and told them all about Immense City and the Giants. As he put on the wig to demonstrate its marvelous power, Ozma looked up at the little Prince in frank admiration.

"You have shown yourself wise and brave and deserve to rule over a Kingdom," said the little Fairy, as Reddy took off the wig and sat down beside her. "I wish I had some of my magic appliances with me, then we could locate the last ruby and restore you to the throne at once. As it is, we'll have to go back to the Emerald City and consult the Wizard of Oz."

"Last ruby," puffed Atmos, who had not paid much attention to the ruby part of the story. "Why, I have a ruby." Reaching in one of his air pockets, the skyman produced a sparkling

square gem. Seizing the jewel with a grasp of surprise, Reddy brought out the other two and held them up for all to see.

"Why, it is the last ruby," cried the little Prince, pointing to the R, carved distinctly on the side of the gem. "It is the ruby that protects me from all danger in the air."

"But how did Atmos get it?" exclaimed Betsy, completely bewildered.

"Well, he is an airman," began Reddy, not quite sure himself, but too surprised and delighted to really care, "And I suppose—"

"I got it from a sky-lark," announced the airman, puffing out his cheeks importantly. "One morning, as I was picking air currents from a large current bush near my air castle, a sky-lark flew by and dropped this ruby into my

196

hand. And as it was bright and shiny, and unlike anything I had ever seen, I kept it."

"Well, good for you!" cried Carter Green, clapping Atmos on the back. "The lark must have caught the ruby as Irashi flung it into the air. Imagine the old scalawag's feelings when he knows that a Vegetable Man found the ruby he buried in the garden, a fisherman the ruby he hurled into the river and an airman, the ruby he tossed into the air! Quite a coincidence, I call it." And taking three skips and a hop to keep from rooting to the spot, Carter perched on a rock he had found himself and began to whistle merrily.

"And now!" exclaimed Betsy, running over to seize Reddy's hands, "Now with all of the rubies you can conquer Irashi and nothing can ever harm you again!"

"Oh, let's go back to Oz," growled the Hungry Tiger, lashing his tail a little at the very thought of Irashi. "Let's go back to Oz where the meals are regular and a tiger's a tiger. Reddy can live with us and we'll all have fun together. That is, if we can ever find a way to cross the desert."

"I'll carry you across," volunteered the airman, looking down at his boots. "I'm big enough and I'd do anything for little Ozma. I'm her airrend boy," he grinned, winking at Carter Green.

"And I'm Betsy's," declared Carter proudly. Jumping off the stone he began hopping round like a jack-rabbit, and Ozma could hardly keep her eyes off the comical little gentleman.

"Let's start, fellows," suggested Carter squinting up at the sun. "Perhaps we are nearer this desert than we think and as we're not sure of the way either to the Emerald City or to Rash, we'll have to go where the next road takes us."

"The desert lies over there," announced Reddy, pointing toward the East. "I saw the gleaming sand when I had on my big wig."

"Then let's go East," sighed Ozma, seating herself contentedly on the Hungry Tiger. In a twinkling Betsy hopped up beside her and with Reddy pacing proudly ahead and Carter and Atmos ambling comfortably behind, the little procession started off.

CHAPTER 19

Reddy Restored to the Throne

THE time passed most merrily for the travellers. Carter and Atmos were so interested in each other, and Betsy and Ozma were so busy exchanging their strange experiences, they scarcely noticed the country through which they were passing. But after an hour's march Reddy, who was still ahead of the others, gave a loud cry of surprise, for he had caught a glimpse of the pink towers of Rash.

"We've travelled in a circle," panted the

little boy excitedly, "and here we are back where we started from."

"Well, shall we stop and conquer Irashi or go on back to Oz?" queried Betsy. "The Deadly Desert is on the other side of the city, and we could easily march around it."

"March round by all means," roared the Hungry Tiger, who had his own reasons for avoiding Rash. "In the Emerald City Ozma can do the whole conquering by magic, and then if Reddy still wants to return to his measly little Kingdom, she can transport him with the Magic Belt."

The little fairy looked inquiringly at Reddy, but Reddy lifted his chin and fingering his sword lovingly, shook his head.

"A Prince should conquer his own enemies," declared the little boy bravely, "and after the way Irashi treated us, I really ought to conquer him."

"But can six people conquer a city?" gasped the airman rolling his eyes a big wildly. "In the sky it takes an army."

"I've seen one person conquer a city in Oz," boasted Betsy proudly. "Come on Red, I'll help you."

"So will I!" cried Carter Green, picking up a stout stick, "And we have the Rash rubies, remember!"

"I don't know much about earth battles, but I can tread on a few toes," offered Atmos, clumping up to the little Prince and tapping his boots significantly.

"And if you are set upon it, I'll bite off a few heads," roared the Hungry Tiger. "On to Rash!" Bidding the little girls hold tight, he went charging full speed over the hill, Reddy, Atmos and Carter racing breathless after him.

Now it happened that Irashi and his Chief Scribe were having luncheon in the castle gardens. They had long since dismissed the Hungry Tiger and the little Prince from their evil minds. You can therefore imagine their astonishment and dismay when Reddy and his companions came hurtling through the trees. The little army had rushed impetuously past the guards at the gate and, after one glimpse of the Hungry Tiger, the Rashers they encountered in the city had fled like leaves before the wind, so that they had reached the castle without interference.

At sight of the huge airman, Ippty, who had been about to pour himself a cup of coffee, gave a frightful scream and scrambled nimbly into a tree, while Irashi, seizing a silver whistle, that hung round his neck, blew three shrill blasts and, drawing his scimiter, made a savage slash at Reddy. But the scimiter slid harmlessly down the little boy's cheek, and the coffee pot, which Ippty hurled from the tree, bounced like a rubber ball, off his head.

"It's the rubies, the Rash rubies!" exulted

201

Betsy Bobbin. Betsy and Ozma had jumped off the tiger, and the great beast, crouched at the foot of Ippty's tree, was glaring upward with a look so terrible that the Scribe of Rash trembled till the very branches shook.

"See what's coming," coughed Carter, with a warning wave toward the castle. In answer to Irashi's whistle, the entire army of Rash was advancing upon the invaders.

"Spinach! Gamin and spinach!" spluttered the Vegetable Man wildly.

"Is that what you call 'em?" panted Atmos, and putting the little girls firmly behind him, he made ready to tread upon the army's toes. Swinging his stick like a flail, Carter took his place at Reddy's right and, roaring like a dozen cannons, the Hungry Tiger placed himself at the little boy's left. Reddy, himself, giving no attention to the frantic slashes of the scimiter, nor the furious advance of the Rash army, was pushing Irashi steadily backwards.

And as the old rascal, breathless from his pummelings, turned to see whether his army were coming, Reddy snatched off Irashi's crown and tossed it back to Betsy Bobbin.

"Keep it for me Betsy," puffed the little Prince, "I can't use it now." Clinging anxiously together, both little girls began to wish they had persuaded Reddy not to conquer Irashi. How was one small boy, even though he was helped out by three magic rubies and five loyal friends, to conquer the entire army of Rash?

But Reddy's plans were all made. As the Rashers rushed upon him, as the airman got in one splendid kick and Carter one tremendous whack, the little boy clapped on the giant's wig.

You have never seen a more terrified and bewildered company. The screams of Irashi and his Guardsmen, as Reddy shot skyward, nearly deafened Betsy and Ozma. And as he began to pick up one and then another of the soldiers and take away their swords, their terror was pitiful. They crawled, ran, leaped, and tumbled in a wild scramble to get away, the Hungry Tiger snapping viciously at their heels and the airman helping them most efficiently with his iron boots. In one moment more, not a Rasher was to be seen anywhere.

"And that," grunted the airman, rubbing his hands together with great glee, "that is the end of the gamin and spinach."

Irashi would have fled too, had not Atmos seized him by the pantaloons and swung him up in the tree beside Ippty. By this time word of the frightful battle had reached the castle and Fizzenpop, his turban standing straight on end, came flying out to see what had happened. But even Fizzenpop's knees smote together when he saw the great Giant striding up and down the garden, and when the Giant actually lifted him into the air, the Grand Vizier gave himself up for lost.

Betsy and Ozma, delighted at the splendid

victory, now came hurrying over and while the Hungry Tiger guarded the two rascals in the tree, Reddy took off his wig, and told Fizzenpop the story of their adventures, proudly displaying the three magic rubies of Rash.

At sight of the rubies, the delight and astonishment of the Grand Vizier knew no bounds, and after embracing Reddy a dozen times and prostrating himself twice before each of the others, the old statesman rushed back to the palace.

Next instant the tower bells were tolling out a joyful welcome to the Rightful Ruler of Rash and, Fizzenpop, himself, in his best turban and tunic was reading a proclamation from the pink balcony stating that Evered, the Scarlet Prince had returned and the rule of Irashi the Rough was over forever.

"How about a little lunch?" proposed the

Hungry Tiger, putting his paws over his ears to drown out the roars and cheers of the populace.

Overjoyed at Irashi's downfall, the citizens of Rash were celebrating the victory as noisily as possible. "And what are we going to do with these two handsome rogues? I've a notion to eat them up!" the Hungry Tiger roared, glaring ferociously at the trembling pair in the tree.

"Well, they certainly deserve it," exclaimed Betsy, looking severely at Irashi and Ippty. "Don't you think so Carter?"

The kind hearted Vegetable Man pulled his corn ear in embarrassment. "Let Ozma and Reddy decide," murmured Carter in a low voice. "They're not an earthly bit of use to anyone, but perhaps they'll reform," he finished uncomfortably. At Carter's words, the airman gave a sudden bounce, and a gleam of purpose came into his round eye.

"Tie them up," advised Atmos, "especially that prickly fingered one. Then, after lunch we can decide what is to be done."

"All right," agreed Reddy, and to be sure that they would not escape, he put on his big wig. Then, picking the two Rashers out of the tree as if they had been toy soldiers, he wound them round and round with rope that Carter obligingly fetched from the castle. Ippty's pen and pencily fingers he bound up securely in strips of his handkerchief, which, grown to giant size, was large as a sheet. Then, with the two culprits tramping gloomily before them, the conquerors marched gaily to the pink palace where a splendid repast already awaited them.

The Hungry Tiger's eyes shone with joy as he looked down the long table. One entire end had been reserved for him.

"Isn't this better than Rash prisoners?" whispered Fizzenpop, leading him kindly to his place and waving to the rare steaks and roasts he had provided.

With a troubled glance at Ozma, the Hungry Tiger nodded. He hoped that Fizzenpop would not tell the others why he had come to Rash. But Betsy and Ozma were talking so busily, they never even heard the Grand Vizier's remark. "And if Ippty and Irashi are disposed of, I have nothing to fear," thought the tiger uneasily.

Reddy, still in his shabby clothes, but wearing the splendid ruby crown of Rash, seated himself at the head of the table and, with Ozma on his right and Betsy on his left, presided in a truly royal manner. Carter and Atmos did not eat at all, but their jokes and questions kept the whole company in a roar of merriment.

"It is seldom," observed old Fizzenpop, gazing fondly at the little Prince, "it is seldom that a city is captured without one broken bone."

"I am glad I did not break mine," said the airman, patting his chest proudly.

"Yours?" gasped Betsy, "Why Atmos, have you any bones?"

"One," admitted the airman, feeling his side experimentally. "It's a floating rib, and I never know just where it will be. Every airman has a floating rib," confided Atmos blandly. "It helps them to float."

"Well, I think you are one of the most interesting persons I have ever met," cried Reddy, jumping to his feet. "And Carter's the other. Oh I do wish you would all stay in Rash. Won't you please stay? Betsy and Ozma can take turns being Queen, Carter can be royal gardener and the Hungry Tiger and Atmos can be anything they want."

"Thanks," murmured the airman, "but what about my lecture? Besides," he looked bashfully from one to the other, "I'm engaged to an Heiress and must return to the sky. But someday, when you have a few years to spare, I hope you'll all visit me and we'll go on a regular sky-lark."

"Oh, I'd love to," cried Betsy Bobbin.

"You talk as if you were leaving us," objected the Hungry Tiger, raising himself with an effort. He had eaten a tremendous luncheon and could scarcely keep his eyes open.

"I am," declared the airman solemnly, pushing back his chair. And before the others half realized what he was about, the huge fellow had seized Ippty and Irashi and vanished through the doorway.

CHAPTER 20

Safe in the Emerald City

"WAIT! Wait!" begged Ozma, jumping up and hurrying after him. "Atmos Fere, Atmos dear, don't you remember you promised to carry us across the desert and back to Oz?" By this time they had all run out into the garden, but Atmos did not even seem to hear their pleas. With Ippty and Irashi under one arm, he was feverishly kicking off his iron boots.

"These villains," puffed Atmos, holding up his unhappy victims, "are as Carter said, of no use on the earth at all, but they will be very useful to me in the sky. Not as good specimens as I could have wished for, but I will take them back with me, to prove that there are really people at the bottom of the air. After the lecture, I shall drop them on some lonely island where they can do no further mischief," declared Atmos calmly.

"Hurrah!" roared the Hungry Tiger, overjoyed that his secret would now be kept safely.

"After the lecture," gasped Ozma faintly, "But that will be years and years by skytime?"

"Years and years," acknowledged Atmos, with a grin, and freeing himself from one boot soared a hundred feet into the air. "Look out below!" he called warningly, "Here comes the other one."

They had just time to dodge aside when the other iron boot came crashing to earth. "Good-bye!" shouted the airman in a faraway voice, "Good-bye, little Princess, I'll see you again, some time!"

"Good-bye!" called Ozma, sadly. Standing on tip-toe, the whole company strained their eyes to catch a last glimpse of their strange fellow adventurer. But Atmos and the two wicked Rashers had already disappeared above the clouds.

"Oh!" wailed Ozma suddenly, "How are we going to cross the Deadly Desert now?"

"Don't cross it," begged Reddy again, "Stay here. Please, stay here!"

"Maybe Dorothy or the Wizard will look in the Magic Picture," suggested Betsy hopefully. "Watch out Carter, you're taking root again."

With a little exclamation of annoyance, the Vegetable Man jerked himself loose and began to comfort the Princess of Oz.

"It was really the best thing that could have happened," he assured her eagerly. "With Irashi and Ippty out of the way, Reddy can rule his Kingdom in peace, and while those two rogues will not really suffer, they will be kept out of mischief for years to come."

"That's so," mused Ozma, thoughtfully, "and I'm rather glad Atmos has some proof. He was such an old dear, when you got to know him."

"You may have my big wig if you wish," offered Reddy, generously, "but I'm afraid, even as a giant, you could not step across the desert."

"No," sighed Ozma, "I suppose not. Besides, every ruler should have at least one magic possession. With the Rash rubies and the giant's wig you ought to be able to rule for many years without any trouble."

"How about the rubies?" asked Carter. "Wouldn't the ruby that protected us from the Gnome King protect us from the burning sands? Why, maybe it was that ruby that helped us to cross the desert in the first place. I had it then, you know!"

211

"I thought it was the quick sandals," said Betsy. "Maybe the ruby would not work on sand Carter and—"

"I have thought of something!" cried Fizzenpop, who was anxious for Reddy to keep all of his magic treasures. "It would be unwise for her Majesty to risk crossing the desert with only the ruby to help her, but with our marvelous canes nothing could harm her at all."

"Canes?" murmured Ozma.

"Hurry canes," smiled the Grand Vizier. "With our patent action, triply guaranteed hurry canes you can all cross the Deadly Desert and safely return to Oz."

"Oh, Fizzenpop!" exclaimed Reddy, in delight, "Why didn't I think of that?"

The Hungry Tiger rolled up his eyes and shuddered, but the others, who had never ridden a Rash hurry cane, were charmed with the Grand Vizier's suggestion. That evening, after Reddy had shown Ozma and the others all over his pretty pink Kingdom, and after the populace had given three cheers for the Rescuers of Rash, Fizzenpop took five hurry canes from the umbrella stand. Five, because at the last minute, Reddy insisted upon going to the Emerald City, too.

Giving Fizzenpop the giant wig, but keeping the Rash rubies himself, and promising to return in a month, Reddy mounted his hurry cane. Then, at a signal from the little Prince, each traveller clapped the head upon his cane and in five furious flashes they were off for Oz, and five minutes later, a little shocked and breathless, dropped down in the Emerald City itself.

Knowing that dear delightful place as you do, you can imagine the welcome accorded the travellers. There were feasts and processions and story tellings and parties enough to satisfy even the Hungry Tiger. For days nothing was talked of, but the marvelous adventures of Betsy Bobbin and the little Princess of Oz. Carter Green was so sought after and invited about, he could not have taken root, even had he wanted to. The little Prince Evered has since returned to his own country, but often comes over to spend a pleasant evening in the castle, bringing along his big wig, to entertain the Scarecrow.

As for the Hungry Tiger, he never drops off to sleep without thanking his stars he is not a kitten, and if at times he looks a little hollow-eyed and wan, he is on the whole happier than ever, for he has learned that it is better to have a stomach-ache than a heart-ache and the heart-aches he had in Rash, missing his friends, cured him forever of the desire to eat a live man.

In the pink palace of Rash the iron boots of Atmos are still shown to visitors, to prove that an airman really visited that country, and on clear nights old Fizzenpop, with a telescope, tries to catch a glimpse of his wicked countrymen.

THE INTERNATIONAL WIZARD OF OZ CLUB

The International Wizard of Oz Club was founded in 1957 to bring together all those interested in Oz, its authors and illustrators, film and stage adaptations, toys and games, and associated memorabilia. From a charter group of 16, the club has grown until today it has over 1800 members of all ages throughout the world. Its magazine, *The Baum Bugle*, first appeared in June 1957 and has been published continuously ever since. The *Bugle* appears three times a year and specializes in popular and scholarly articles about Oz and its creators, biographical and critical studies, first edition checklists, research into the people and places within the Oz books, etc. The magazine is illustrated with rare photographs and drawings, and the covers are in full color. The Oz Club also publishes a number of other Oz-associated items, including full-color maps; an annual collection of original Oz stories; books; and essays.

Each year, the Oz Club sponsors conventions in different areas of the United States. These gatherings feature displays of rare Oz and Baum material, an Oz quiz, showings of Oz films, an auction of hard-to-find Baum and Oz items, much conversation about Oz in all its aspects, and many other activities.

The International Wizard of Oz Club appeals to the serious student and collector of Oz as well as to any reader interested in America's own fairyland. For further information, please send a *long* self-addressed stamped envelope to:

Fred M. Meyer, Executive Secretary
THE INTERNATIONAL WIZARD
   OF OZ CLUB
Box 95
Kinderhook, IL 62345